HAVEN

GENESHIFTERS BOOK THREE

REBECCA LEMKE

This book is a work of fiction. Any reference to historical events, real people, or real locales are used fictitiously. Other names, characters, places, and incidents are products of the author's imagination, and any resemblance to actual events or locales or persons, living or dead, is entirely coincidental.

First Edition, May 2025

Anatole Publishing

Summary: When a comrade and the mad scientist the Titans were holding captive go missing, they go to rescue the both of them and get more than they bargained for.

ISBN 978-0-9990593-6-4 (paperback) / 978-0-9990593-7-1 (hardback)

[1. Genetic engineering—Fiction. 2. Adventure and adventurers—Fiction. 3. Science fiction.]

Book Layout © 2021 BookDesignTemplates.com
Book Cover Design by Deranged Doctor Design
Editing by Bird and Bear Editoral Services

This book is dedicated to my readers, who have patiently waited for nearly three years for this book. Thank you for your unwavering love and support!

" 'Cause in my head there's a greyhound station
Where I send my thoughts to far off destinations
So they may have a chance of finding a place
Where they're far more suited than here..."

— Death Cab for Cutie, "Soul Meets Body"

CHAPTER ONE

THE LITTLE GIRL

"Что с ней не так?"

[What's wrong with her?]

"Я не знаю, она всегда такая."

[I don't know; she's always like that.]

"Пора идти, детка. Вставай."

[Time to go, baby. Get up.]

A little girl sat in the corner, hugging her knees. She wore a blank expression on her face as she stared down at the red patterned carpet, stained with time and wear.

It was hard to tell how old she was because, while she was small, she was very intelligent. Was she a precocious six-year-old, or a gaunt eight-year-old? The orphanage workers didn't know. Nor did they care.

Grime clung to her skin and matted hair. Particularly on her face where she had brushed away her bangs over and over again. Her body was prone to repetitive motion, they had noticed. It was curious. *She* was curious.

Her arrival wasn't unusual. Not compared to anyone else's. Dropped on the doorstep, abandoned.

She did act a bit more traumatized than the rest of the children, but it was hard to say what could be the cause of that since she never spoke. Perhaps she didn't know their mother tongue. Or perhaps she was deaf, or maybe mute. Maybe she just chose not to speak at all.

Whatever the reason behind her silence, it persisted.

The girl didn't move, and so the elder of the orphanage workers moved to pick the child up.

She lifted the young one into the air and started toward the door. She could not fathom what would cause someone to adopt the most difficult case in the orphanage, and she had mixed feelings about the girl's departure. While she was hard to take care of and perpetually scared, she was very, very sweet if you were kind to her.

"Что это такое?" [What is it?] The younger of the workers pointed to the child's neck, at a spot now exposed, where her hair had fallen before.

"Этот?" [This?] the elder responded, pointing to the area on her skin.

"Шрам, я думаю," [Scar, I think,] she followed up.

"Странный." [Strange.] The younger shuddered.

The elder had always assumed that the girl had been in a fire. It would make sense considering her skittishness. Unfortunately, some people were very vain, and it was possible she had been given away due to the scar. Though, the spot did not resemble a normal burn. It was almost scaly. Many of the workers in the orphanage refused to touch her because they believed she had some sort of leprosy.

The elder woman preferred to believe that if it was a burn, she was given up because her parents perished and not because they no longer thought she was worth caring for.

Whatever it was that had caused it, the skin on the child's neck was unusually textured and discolored. Though, it did not seem to hurt the child to touch.

A knock came at the door, causing the girl to cling to her. She didn't know if the child could hear the knock, or if the little one had felt her flinch. Either way, she was now burrowing into her caretaker's shoulder like her life depended on it. Her heart wrenched as she felt the little girl's tummy rise and fall with stress.

If she could stop time and just think things through, she would in a heartbeat. She didn't know if this was the right thing to do for this little girl. But she felt in her very soul that the child's life was about to change.

The younger woman rushed to the door to open it. Time moved as though it had been sped up, in the elder's mind.

A youthful man with dark sunglasses strode into their humble orphanage, wearing shiny shoes and a tailored suit. This wasn't their normal sort of patron, but maybe his wife was barren? Infertility took all kinds, they knew. It was not hers to judge, so she put on a smile and welcomed the man.

She couldn't see where his eyes went behind his glasses, but his white teeth were displayed freely in a smile. While it didn't make her uncomfortable, it also didn't put her at ease.

"это мой новый ребенок," [This is my new baby,] the man said cheerily.

The elder was impressed by his speech, as he did not look like he would speak their mother tongue. She was prepared to have someone translate.

"Да," [Yes,] the young woman said.

He beamed at the girl, and at the two women.

"я позабочусь о ней," [I will take care of her,] the man told the women proudly.

They went to sit down and fill out paperwork. When the ink was dry, the elder woman's throat felt just as much so. The man reached out to take the reluctant child from her arms, and as he pulled her away, she silently cried and looked into the elder woman's eyes.

The elder woman's body ached as she held back tears of her own and watched as the man took the child down the very steps they'd found her on, onto the street, and into a black car.

"счастлив избавиться от нее," [Happy to be rid of her,] the younger woman said before walking off.

The elder woman shut the orphanage door as the car disappeared down the street, and when it was closed, she let herself cry.

CHAPTER 2

TREVOR AND MIRANDA

"Is there anything else I can get for you?" The waitress held her pen, poised to write, as she spoke.

"I think that's everything," Miranda said sweetly, stealing a glance at Trevor.

He nodded, smiling at Miranda, then at the waitress.

"Alrighty, I'll be right back with your drinks!"

"Thank you," Trevor told her, before she disappeared behind him toward the kitchen in the little diner.

Miranda still had a good view of the waitress when she went past the doors and into the kitchen. The little window in the door revealed the woman speaking with a coworker, and she swiped three fingers across her face. She looked quizzical but then nodded at whatever the coworker had said to her. Miranda sank down into the red leather booth seat.

She suddenly felt self-conscious. Her whiskers had more than once gotten her looks, but people usually mumbled something about "cosplaying" and moved on. Still…it was embarrassing. She knew she should be thankful that was all the response it elicited. Walking openly as herself was a luxury afforded her in this sanctuary city. And for that, she was grateful.

She could get rid of the whiskers, of course. They were the first step in going from human toward transforming into the cat her DNA had been spliced with in the Titan program. The fact that her hair had started to change to calico coloring didn't seem to go away by reverting to fully human, but the whiskers were easy. The problem was, whenever she completely changed to human, her cat allergies kicked back in. Hard.

So, her two choices were this compromise, or be fully human while sneezing her head off constantly. She supposed turning all the way into a cat constituted a third option, but she couldn't exactly go out to eat with her boyfriend as a cat. He *was* her boyfriend…wasn't he? Miranda thought he was.

Trevor grinned at her, reaching out for her hand.

"This is nice." His eyes twinkled, and though his face had hardened over the past year, he looked younger than ever. So much so that she could almost believe he'd gotten over Isaac, their friend who had died during a rescue mission.

"It is." Miranda forced a smile that was brighter than how she really felt. It seemed like the closer to normalcy they got, the more she was reminded that they couldn't have it.

Trevor didn't believe that, though.

"This could be our all-the-time." He tried to look into her eyes, but she found the menu suddenly fascinating. He pressed on as she memorized the bread options for sandwiches and spices in the sauces.

"I want that for us," Trevor continued earnestly, "and I'm not afraid to say it. We can't live our lives afraid. The people here say there are towns out there, even ones like this one. The world is so much bigger than we thought, full of so many opportunities and—"

He broke off abruptly as the bell of the diner door chimed. Their heads turned in unison as a well-dressed man with a large mustache walked in and sauntered up to the counter.

The waitress hurried out of the kitchen to greet him.

"Oh, hello! We don't have an open table at the moment, but…"

She paused as he held up a glimmering card.

"Oh! I'm so sorry, I should have remembered that you were a Haven Club member. I'll take you back right away."

The waitress stepped out from behind the counter and escorted the man around the corner on the far side of the diner from Miranda and Trevor, after which they disappeared from view.

Trevor turned back to Miranda and rolled his eyes.

"Well, that was obnoxious."

"It was?" Miranda replied, partly grateful that the distraction had caused Trevor to let go of her hand, but also partly missing his touch. Her feelings about this dating thing were really going to take some getting used to. And straightening out.

"I mean, do you not think these Haven Club people are obnoxious?" asked Trevor. "They get all these special perks and free stuff and—"

"We've been given an allowance by Mayor Cassandra since we moved here; we technically get perks and free stuff, too," Miranda reminded him.

"Yeah, but we're not snooty like them," said Trevor, though the air had been taken out of the rant he was winding up to. "They just act like they're better than everyone else," he finished lamely.

"Don't let it bother you," soothed Miranda, voice moving into a whisper. "You have something special that they could never have."

Trevor looked at her quizzically and whispered back, "Lizard DNA?"

"No!" groaned Miranda, embarrassedly cringing as it came out a bit too much like a cat yowl. "Me for a girlfriend!"

Trevor's Adam's apple bobbed as he swallowed, trying to come up with some way of recovering.

Just then, a persistent, high-pitched squeak came rushing through the restaurant. His eyes went wide and he searched around to find the source. Miranda sighed knowingly. She didn't know whether to thank Natalie for saving her from Trevor's attempt to save face or be upset that she had crashed their date. Natalie strode up in human form from behind a counter that housed condiments, paper towels, and a hidden trash can. A napkin fell haphazardly from her head.

Trevor's jaw briefly dropped, but he quickly closed it to avoid drawing attention to them.

"What are you doing here?" he said in a low voice. If he had talked to Miranda that way, she would've felt it was threatening or mad, but Natalie brushed it off. She was panting heavily, bracing her hands on her knees. Transforming from mouse to human was taxing enough, but she must have been running before that, too.

Miranda's eyebrows furrowed. "Are you okay?" she asked. Natalie looked disturbed, and she couldn't tell if it was from breathlessness alone or if something was wrong.

"Luna," Natalie puffed, looking at them through the hair falling in her face, "and Silen…are gone."

The last remains of Trevor's joy and hope slipped from his face like glass and shattered on the floor into a million pieces. "What do you mean '*gone*'?"

"Kidnapped," Natalie puffed out, her small frame racked by the effort as she pointed toward the door. "Adam's back, and he's working on a plan now."

Miranda watched the indecision war in Trevor's mind. Go and choose to be right back in that mess or decide this was someone else's problem.

Something won out, and she didn't know what it was until he stood up and tossed a few bills on the counter.

"I'm going to help," he told her through gritted teeth. "You stay here, stay safe, and enjoy eating my ice cream." Then he scrambled out the door.

Miranda crestfallen, both at the bad news and at Trevor's departure, barely managed a wave as the confused waitress returned with their drinks.

Natalie sat down across from Miranda.

"*Soooo*, since the boys have got this…can I have some ice cream, too?"

CHAPTER 3

JAMES

If you want to see them again, you'll bring James to me.

Alive.

The tracker will show you the way.

The words on the paper burned themselves into my brain. My eyes blurred as the note faded out of focus and the pavement of the street replaced it as a focal point.

Adam's jaw worked as everyone scrambled around him. Titania's big brown eyes looked close to crying. Melody was visibly distraught as well. She sat quietly in her wheelchair while nervously fiddling with the blanket that covered her long fish tail. We'd just gotten back from the underwater facility.

So many questions were running through my brain: Who was going? Should we use the tracker left with the note? Was it a trap? Why did they want me, and how did they even know my name? Had Silen given it? None of it made sense.

I shook my head; we all needed to focus. And I needed more medicine to stave off the radiation poisoning.

Jen conferred with Adam on logistics, but he looked like he wasn't hearing a word of it.

I put my hand on Adam's shoulder, and he seemed even more of a mountain of a man than usual. His height was imposing enough to begin with, but even more so when he turned to me. I could see the wild in his eyes. If he could think clearly, I would be shocked. Luna was everything to him.

At the very least, he and I were going. There was no way he wasn't chasing after Luna, and I was named in the ransom note.

"Let's go to the office and take stock. We need to refresh supplies," I suggested.

Adam broke into a run, and I picked up my pace to match him. The girls trailed behind us. How was he not tired after everything we'd been through recently? Adrenaline was a powerful thing, but I was exhausted.

He raced into the gym, passing the crazy little kids that bounced off the walls, and beelined to his office in the back. Adam yanked the door open and started scrambling through his belongings that were scattered across the table. Then he swiveled around and started digging through a cabinet. I stood, hands at my side, waiting to be told what to do or how to help.

Adam threw some material that had been originally intended for Titania's fireproof suit, and it landed squarely on the table behind him. The sudden movement made me a little queasy. Everything was moving so fast…

Titania caught up to us first, and she flipped on the light when she arrived. I felt my stomach churn, and then its contents were on the floor.

She gasped. "Are you okay?"

I wasn't sure. That was awfully sudden. Emphasis on the *awful* part.

Adam was above me in a flash, and gone was his dissociative expression and rage.

"I'm sorry, man." His brown eyes were soft and full of concern. He handed me another pill like he had when we'd entered the underwater compound just days ago.

"You definitely got radiation poisoning." He grimaced.

I popped the bright pill in my mouth and swallowed it dry. I needed it to work immediately.

"Maybe I should take him to rest before you head out," Titania said.

It came out more as a demand than a suggestion.

Adam nodded, agreeing. I didn't want to hold him up, but I could hardly see straight. We had come speeding home from the underwater compound where we had searched in vain for the antidote to our condition as Titans. I had flown the whole way back in winged-lion form and hadn't slept in about two days. I needed a break.

Titania put her shoulder under my armpit and walked me out of the room, and Adam flipped off the light as we left and passed in front of all the kids.

"*Ewwwww*, he looks *greeen*." A little girl pointed at me.

"Sh, that's not nice," Titania scolded her. "He's sick."

"AHHHHH!!" The little girl ran away, and all of the Titan children around her did the same. I groaned at the annoyance, but at least we had a clear path now.

We stepped over the threshold of the facility and I felt the same unsettling sensation in my throat, but held it at bay. I couldn't throw up the pill. While Adam was certainly resourceful, we didn't have infinite resources. And the sooner the medicine hit my system, the sooner I'd feel better.

Titania's eyes surveyed me with anxiety.

"I'm fine," I lied through my teeth.

She glared at me and sped toward the apartments. It was like playing a game of three-legged race, except it was against my will.

I tried to focus on Cassandra's tower in the distance. The hub of the city, where everything was decided and everyone important resided. If I chose to keep my eyes on something stable and unmoving, then I hoped I could keep the contents of my stomach in.

The blocks felt like miles, and Titania's pensive expression was stressing me out. I would be okay. If I'd made it through being transformed into a Titan, being spliced with two different animals, I could make it through this.

I took a deep breath when we approached the elevator at the apartment. Would it make me motion sick? Maybe if I closed my eyes…

I heard the doors open right before the familiar voice of Greg echoed out.

"Whoa, is he okay?" asked our middle-aged neighbor.

I felt Titania's muscles tense.

"Yeah, he's just kinda nauseous."

"Oh no!" Greg exclaimed. "Did he eat at the taco place down the street? I'm telling you, I get food poisoning every time I eat there! Do you need help getting him to his apartment? I'll stay with you…"

He rambled on, but I couldn't focus on his words. Titania sounded like she was trying to put up resistance, but we both knew that was useless. This was Greg we were talking about. He wrapped his arm under my other armpit and hauled me into the elevator with Titania. I peeked my eye open just a little to nod and thank him.

The trip up the few floors to my apartment was excruciating, but my door was a welcome sight. How long had we been gone for? I couldn't even think clearly.

Titania left Greg propping me up while she unlocked the door, shoving it open. Greg hauled me to the couch and set me down, more gently than I anticipated he would, for which I was grateful. Titania shooed him out, politely, while he rambled his offers of home remedies for food poisoning. The silence in the room upon the door shutting was a welcome relief.

Titania quickly rushed to my side, feeling my forehead. She then flew to the kitchen and brought back a bowl, placing it on the coffee table.

"In case you feel like you're going to throw up again," she said, then winced. She looked at the papers lying all around the table and began scooping them up and setting them in a stack on the other end, away from any potential projectiles.

"Thanks." I grimaced. This was embarrassing.

Titania stood and paced the room. I shut my eyes, willing the wooziness away. It wasn't working.

"Are you sure you ought to be going?" She turned to me, her brown eyes shimmering with concern.

I groaned, "I don't think it would be good for Adam to go alone. He might take out anything and everything to get to Luna."

Titania contemplated. She nodded, knowingly.

"Promise me you'll be careful?" Her eyes shown with moisture.

My heart squeezed as I realized she was about to cry. I couldn't have that.

"Of course I'll be careful." I reached out for her hand and she reluctantly let me take it.

She scowled.

"I'm serious. It'll be okay," I assured her.

She broke away, mulling it over as she resumed picking up the papers and straightening them into a perfect square to put in a nearby box.

"Can I see those?" I asked, holding my head and sitting up.

Titania walked them to me and handed the stack over.

My face heated as I realized that they were the letters I'd written her while she was dead. In the year when her phoenix DNA hadn't brought her back to life yet.

"Are you okay? You look flushed!" Terror washed over her face and she threw the bowl at me.

"Yeah," I said sheepishly. "It's just the letters from when you were gone."

She paused.

"I thought you'd burned them all," she murmured.

"No, not all," I whispered as I flipped through them.

In that moment, I knew I had a choice to make. I could brush all this aside and hide them, disposing of them when I got back from rescuing Luna and Silen, or...

"I want you to have them." I pushed them toward her.

"What?" Her eyes went wide.

"It's all stuff I wanted to say to you. I used to go into the woods, remembering how much you loved running through the woods when we were kids, and let the ghost of you take me away for a while."

"But you burned some because you didn't want me seeing them," she said, biting her lip.

"I was young and dumb," I said playfully, by way of apology.

She smirked. "You were seventeen."

"And now," I countered, "I'm seventeen and some change. It's called character growth!"

"Are you sure?" Her dark eyes surveyed the pile of papers before turning their captivating charm on me.

"Yes, under one condition…" I smiled, pulling her down so her face was in front of me.

"What's that?" she asked hesitantly.

"Don't read them until Adam and I have left," I said quietly, leaning forward and kissing her on her forehead.

She sighed.

CHAPTER 4

TREVOR

Trevor walked away from the café, mumbling under his breath. His date with Miranda had been going so well. Why did everything always have to be ruined by this stupid Titan stuff? Why couldn't they all just lay low and keep their heads down? Nobody had to know they weren't completely human!

He ran a hand angrily through his spiked hair as he made his way down the street. He didn't even care if the few people loitering noticed him having a moment. He was one irritated dude out of a whole city of people. Better to be having a bad day on his own than taking it out on someone else.

The gym soon came into sight. It was part of an old, abandoned recreation center that Cassandra had allowed them to use to house Titan children that they had rescued. Thankfully, it was still connected to the power grid and had running water, even though it was so far on the outskirts of Reunion City that few ventured there anymore.

Trevor's mind raced. How could Luna be gone? She was literally a wolf! He wouldn't pick a fight with her for anything. As much as he wanted to stay out of it…this was *Luna*.

He grasped the handle of the door and swung it open a little too forcefully. It made a loud noise as it struck the outside wall. The gym was bustling with kids, and now every single one of them was looking at him. He gulped.

This place was the hub, and that made it the first place to look when stuff was going down. He knew he was in the right place for answers, he just needed to find someone over four feet tall.

Jen appeared around the corner, right on time, with a Titan toddler on her hip.

"Having fun playing house?" he quipped as he surveyed the madhouse of children swarming the both of them.

"Playing?" Jen shot back. "I'd love to see you try to 'play' house."

Trevor tried to pat a child that had clung to his leg, but it latched onto his hand with its teeth.

"Ouch!" he yelped.

Jen cackled as she walked away.

Trevor blushed and wiggled out of the grasp of the child, causing it to burst into tears. He booked it as fast as he could to Adam's office.

The door was cracked open. He tried to peek inside but couldn't see Adam, so he pushed the door all the way open.

Adam stood in the dark room, his lips pensively drawn.

"Hey, man," Trevor said tentatively. "I just heard the news."

Adam turned his gaze to Trevor, and his heart dropped. Adam's eyes were filled with a dark, endless fury.

Trevor knew Adam and Luna were close, but he didn't know how close exactly. And he was starting to think he had underestimated their relationship.

"I'm coming with you to get her," Trevor said, swallowing hard.

As much as he didn't want to face all of this Titan stuff, he would never *ever* pass up an opportunity to repay Luna for the debt he owed her. He knew that he wasn't the only Titan who owed her their life.

Adam sighed, sitting down at his desk and pouring over what looked like supplies he'd been packing.

"I don't know what we're walking into," Adam said, his voice unreadable. Was he trying to talk Trevor out of this? Gauge if his offer was just lip service?

"I don't need to know," Trevor said earnestly. "It doesn't matter. I owe her everything I have."

Adam's lips curved up into a sad, tired smile. He nodded. He seemed to know that Luna's legacy, though not what he wanted for her, was a legacy nonetheless. Of idealistic advocacy, even when it endangered herself. The risks she took were great, but Trevor would make sure that the lives she'd saved wouldn't go to waste.

"Do you know who took her?" Trevor asked anxiously. He didn't really want to tussle with more scientists with tranquilizers.

Adam wordlessly tossed a paper onto the table. Trevor leaned over it and read.

He frowned.

"Why would they want James?" He was such a new addition compared to the rest of them, it seemed odd to Trevor to have him as the ransom.

"I don't know." Adam folded his hands under his chin. "But we at least know that it is someone who knows who James is and finds him to be of value to them."

"Maybe it's Silen," Trevor ventured. "He's gone too, right? Maybe he escaped and took Luna as a hostage."

"I don't think Silen is that competent," Adam said through a suppressed chuckle. "Plus, the ransom note says 'if you want to see *them* again,' not just her."

"Well, if we're not dealing with Silen, who could we be dealing with?" Trevor began to pace. He didn't like the unknowns.

Adam turned the tracker over in his hands, inspecting it for any distinctive markings or emblems.

"Is it branded?" Trevor pointed to the tracker.

"No," Adam sighed. "I suspect it is homemade."

Trevor's face dropped. The government would use one of their standard, run-of-the-mill trackers, even if it was a little outdated. If it wasn't one of those, that meant…

"Some kind of vigilante?"

Adam tilted his head as he considered this. "I don't know of any enemies we have outside of the government."

"What are we waiting for?" Trevor asked impatiently. He didn't like open loops. He needed answers. He needed Luna.

"James, actually," Adam said. "We can't exactly leave without the person being demanded."

"But…" Adam continued, seeing that Trevor's barely contained energy was pushing him out the door, "he has radiation poisoning. I gave him something to counteract it, but he does need to rest overnight."

"Oh, come on!" Trevor whined. "He can sleep on the way there!"

Adam raised an eyebrow. "He was vomiting. Are you sure you want to ride with that situation?"

Trevor turned a little green, much the same color as his lizard skin in Titan form.

"Plus," Adam added, "Titania insisted. I don't know about you, but I am not up for arguing with her about James' safety. I don't have a death wish."

CHAPTER 5

TREVOR

The next morning, Trevor paced impatiently outside of the gym, waiting for Adam. If he could've worn a path in the concrete, he would have.

Jen wouldn't let him in, saying he needed to wait here or he was gonna wake the babies. Even after he'd protested that he'd be quiet, she'd fixed him with a glare and shut the door. She had even locked it! He'd gently tried to open it, only to find it wouldn't budge. Jen was protective of all the younger Titans housed in the gym. Due to its location, it was the perfect place to hide a gaggle of human-animal hybrids without drawing too much attention.

The sky was still dark, with a touch of nip in the air. It felt kinda nice, being alone in the stillness. Then he considered it might just be the calm before the storm. He needed to get to Luna!

He raised his hand to bang on the gym door, disregarding what Jen had said, but it moved just as his knuckles would've made impact with the metal.

"…and the medical kit is on the table, try not to need it." Adam's voice was low as he rattled off last-minute instructions to Jen before turning to face the outside.

Adam looked at him, eyebrow raised as his hand hovered in the air. Trevor sheepishly returned it to his side.

"Sorry, I'd just like to get a move on."

Adam nodded wordlessly and moved forward, tossing a final wave back at Jen. Jen shut the door. Trevor heard the click of the lock as they started walking down the road toward the middle of town. It was deafeningly quiet, save for the sound of their footsteps.

Trevor caught a glimpse of Adam's eyes as they passed the last buzzing streetlight outside of the apartment complex. They were bloodshot. Had he slept at all?

The silence stretched on through the elevator ride and down the hall. Adam knocked on James' door, then brushed some of the hair from out of his eyes.

The door swung open, and they were greeted by the sight of James trying to pull on boots in the near dark.

"I'm almost ready," he whispered, snatching a backpack from the ground.

"No more nausea?" Adam asked.

James grimaced as he stepped out. "Only a little. Titania kept coming by to check on me throughout the night, until she ended up falling asleep in the recliner."

The sound of rushing footsteps echoed out of the apartment unit, and Titania came into view. She looked almost as bad as Adam did, Trevor thought.

"Bye," she murmured, burying her face into James' chest. He wrapped his arms around her and held her for a moment.

Trevor folded his arms and smirked, but Adam looked away, giving them some privacy. James stroked her hair, whispered something neither of them could hear, and she reluctantly let go.

"We'll be back soon," James told her as he crossed the threshold. "I promise."

They left her there, in the dark doorway, and set out for Luna.

CHAPTER 6

LUNA

"What do you think they want from us?" I fell back into the chair in frustration. Blonde wisps of hair hung in my eyes, but with my hands restrained I couldn't do anything about it. The wall-to-wall blankness of the white room was maddening.

Silen was unusually contemplative and quiet. That made me more anxious than anything else in the situation. If Silen wasn't being a pest, there was something wrong. His face was blank, and he barely moved. I thought he was ignoring me as the empty moments ticked by. I closed my eyes, deciding to rest for whatever might come next.

Silen's voice was clear but lacking energy when he finally spoke.

"We're well beyond me knowing the players in this game or what their motivations are."

Part of the reason we'd kept Silen alive was intel, and that was more limited than I would've liked.

"Regardless of how you all…" He paused before continuing, "…you *Titans* conceive of yourselves, in everyone else's eyes, you're government property. Political pieces on a chessboard for both the government and its enemies, should you fall into their hands. Now, what our present company is, is yet to be—" The door opened, cutting him off before he could finish the sentence.

"Having a little powwow in here, are we?" the boss of this stupid outfit, a guy in his late teens, asked as he strode in. The boy who had taken us captive, who I guessed to be about fifteen, came in at his heels.

That younger one seemed like he was just a kid. But weren't we all? What did that really mean in the grand scheme of things here? But I was a human-wolf hybrid, and he'd been able to get the jump on me and load me and a full-grown crazed scientist up in his All-Terrain Contactless Vehicle and cart us to who knows where…Props. I had to give him props.

Even after I'd woken up, no one had forbidden me and Silen from talking to each other. That seemed uncharacteristic for kidnappers. My mind suddenly considered the possibility that it was because they wanted to listen to our conversations. Did these people have that capacity? I'd wondered, too, why they hadn't separated us. We'd have to be careful with our words lest we give away important information to these goons.

"What's the matter?" the boss purred. "Cat got your tongue? I hope I didn't interrupt anything important…"

I growled, letting my vocal cords shift just slightly to wolf.

"Oh, that's right. You're a dog. Sorry." He laughed.

Silen laughed too, stopping only when I glared at him.

"Don't worry," the young man said in a way that was almost reassuring, if it weren't for the fact that we were tied up. "I know you miss your friends. It looks like they are on their way."

He held up a device with a screen that blinked green with a circular graph and a dot. I cursed Adam inwardly, knowing that he was likely leading this charge because of me. I wished he would just trust me to find a way out on my own. I could do it, I just needed to come up with a plan.

The young man seemed pleased with my irritation and uncertainty. But he didn't seem to have the malice that most of the people we'd encountered had. Who was he?

I looked directly into his eyes, and he didn't look away. He simply watched me, just as curiously as I watched him.

CHAPTER 7

THE LITTLE GIRL

The little girl sat in the corner, curled up in a ball. She hadn't made eye contact with him or spoken a word on the initial drive home from the orphanage. She hadn't wanted to get out of the car, but she wouldn't let him touch her.

So he left the car and front door open until it got dark out and she decided she was more scared of that than she was of him.

She had been this way since he had brought her home weeks ago, withdrawn and sullen. He had hoped that she would come out of her shell, but the orphanage had warned him that she was quiet and kept to herself.

He had also hoped to be able to make her useful. Perhaps she could be taught domestic responsibilities and her unique… *marking*…would be a fun party trick to show guests. For a price, of course. But if all else failed, he'd send her to his contact in America, if they wanted her. There were lots of people interested in unusual humans, and Americans seemed particularly obsessed. Movies, TV shows, and books all boasted humans that looked different, sounded different, acted different, or were uniquely gifted.

He sat a blanket next to her spot in the corner, locked the door, and turned off the light.

"Good night, little monster," he said in Russian before retreating to his own bedroom, leaving her alone.

"She still isn't talking?" the visitor asked the well-dressed man as they carried out their conversation in Russian.

He was silent for a long moment, then drew himself up with a sigh and quietly said, "No."

"Perhaps she is mute? Didn't the orphanage say that is what they suspected?"

"Yes," the man said simply, standing from his chair and walking toward his guest. He picked up a glass of caramel-colored liquid with ice, taking a sip.

"But you don't believe that?" the guest asked incredulously. "Isn't that the most obvious explanation?"

"Perhaps." The man set the glass down, staring once again at the object of all of his curiosity for the last several weeks. Despite living in a home with the child, he knew very little about her. While most things that looked a little strange could garner attention, and she certainly was strange with her interesting markings, her quietness kept her under the radar, even for those who wanted to learn more about her. It was almost as if one could forget she was even there. His plan of using her as a freak show exhibit was quickly falling by the wayside. It was hard to have a spectacle that was as quiet as a mouse.

The girl didn't look over at them, but the man knew that she was listening. A gnawing wish to know the information that her mind held tore at his insides. She, this silent child, incited anger in him. He couldn't explain it. It wasn't the money he had sunk into her, although she *had* been sold to him for a pretty penny from the orphanage. No, it was more than that. He knew she was significant. Somehow. But he couldn't shake the feeling that he might never know how. Regardless, he couldn't keep her. She hadn't been a good investment for him and he needed to recoup his money.

"I think I'll sell her. I have a buyer in America that is chomping at the bit to acquire her."

"Why is that?" The guest leaned back in his chair, spreading his legs comfortably.

"I don't know," the man said, pinching the bridge of his nose. He didn't want to think about the answer to that question, honestly. While he was upset that the child hadn't been what he had hoped in terms of return on investment, he didn't want to see her hurt. Not that he had any reason to believe that the American buyer would injure her. After all, she was a child. But he found his instincts and anxiety ran on the same track in his mind, and it was hard to differentiate the two.

"Perhaps for science," he posited, if only to make himself feel better. "Perhaps they would like to learn how to make her scars heal."

"That would be a noble undertaking," the guest said, swallowing hard as he stole a glance at the girl who was staring a hole in the wall in the corner.

"Yes." The man comforted himself with that possibility. "It would."

The ship was unstable, rocking back and forth. And yet, the child was stationary the entire way, only moving when required to. Apart from a few of the mushy apples she was offered, and some bread, she ate like a bird. Not a word was uttered to anyone by her. Though the staff did enough muttering about her to last a lifetime, all of which she heard, even if they didn't realize that she understood what they were saying. At least the ones who spoke her mother tongue.

Many people regarded her with confusion, contempt, and frustration. It was intense how much the silent child could incense her caregivers by being largely unresponsive. With each passing day, she seemed more downtrodden. The ship's doctor was called on more than one occasion, not only to check on her appetite, but also on the unusual markings that seemed to only grow along her skin. The doctor shoved a camera in her face, holding her roughly by the arm as he took pictures of her skin.

When he let her go, she curled back up into the tiniest ball she could form and went back into her own little world.

The staff upon the boat knew what destiny was awaiting her on the American shore. And while some pitied her, others hoped that she would escape the fate that they feared. But in the end, there was nothing they could do. Or rather, nothing they *would* do.

The air was cold when she was led out of her cabin, which was little more than a prison cell with a port window, and onto the deck of the ship like all of the other cargo. One of the women who worked in the kitchen gave her an apple while tears sprang from her eyes. One last parting gift. The woman feared the girl wouldn't last long, but she hoped to be wrong.

Gloomy clouds covered the canvas of sky that expanded before her. When she looked up, she felt even smaller than she already did. She trudged along, guided by an elderly man who had been tasked with trading her over to her new owner.

A woman appeared. A pretty woman. But, like many pretty women, this one seemed to the child to have a hidden meanness. Reluctantly, she took the new woman's hand and watched as papers were passed between the two adults. The man didn't speak her mother tongue, and neither did the woman. Fear overtook her as she realized she could no longer understand what was going on around her. She would no longer know what was being said about her, what the plans for her future would be. She was, for the very first time, completely alone and isolated.

She began to cry in the middle of the gray, dull street. The woman bent down to shush her, which did nothing to alleviate her fears. She only stopped crying because she feared what the woman would do if she didn't.

A shiny, overly opulent vehicle awaited the two of them. Just like before, the little girl was ushered inside with no idea what to expect from her new owner. Would she be like the man, who, while long-suffering, would eventually lose interest in her and sell her to someone else? She knew the concept of a pet. The orphanage had once had a pet dog. She wondered if she was a pet. Were there other little kids that adults kept as pets? She had heard rumblings at her previous owner's home. Did other adults keep each other as pets? She didn't think that she wanted to be a pet. She knew some kids did not have to be pets. But they usually spoke, and she didn't. It wasn't that she couldn't speak.

At least, she *thought* she could. But no one could hear her. And when she tried to speak, she only heard it in her own mind.

The woman dipped into the back seat of the car, motioning for the little girl to follow. The child looked out to the open street, contemplating for a second what would happen if she ran away. She'd overheard stories of pets running away. But she didn't know how she would take care of herself if she did that. At least the people she'd been with had known that sometimes she was hungry, or sometimes she needed water. She knew that there was a currency to life that she couldn't navigate on her own. And so, she took a step into the car. Into a new life with a new owner.

CHAPTER 8

ALAN

It was best to not ask questions. It was best to keep your head down.

It was best to not find yourself in the wrong room, in the wrong crowd.

Every sane person knew this. Every sane person abided by these general rules of thumb.

But I had never done what was best. And while I could arguably be called *insane*, sometimes, trouble just found me. Sometimes it was through no fault of my own that I found myself where I was not meant to be.

I had been down in the sewers. Not the most pleasant place to be, for sure. But there were few people still around who seemed to care about the environment. To care about what the biological warfare that had been unleashed on us had done to us. I was one such person.

The sewers beneath Reunion City were a wealth of knowledge, for those who cared to look. Not only because of the unusual algae that grew there, or the unique bacterial and mineral content of the sewage itself, but also because I always managed to find something unexpected on my trips.

Nothing could've been more unexpected than finding a room full of people making a ruckus after midnight when I was trying to find a sample to swab from the wall. I had been so focused on finding the perfect specimen that I had traveled far lower than I'd intended and wandered into something I'd never expected.

I immediately was out of place in my tattered button-down, hair that I probably hadn't remembered to brush, and slacks that had seen far better days. But before I could find my sense to be self-conscious, something captured my attention. Or rather, some*one*.

In the middle of the room, beneath a high, dome-like ceiling, was an arena. And inside of the arena, there seemed to be creatures that I only had vague clearance to know about at my day job.

Titans.

At least, I suspected. Why else would a humanoid-looking creature have wings? Or a tail?

What was held inside of that arena was certainly not fully human. My breath caught in my chest as I froze in place. This was far more than I could take in. Was I dreaming? Hallucinating? Had I inhaled a little too much of the dusty blue mold that I had scraped off a pipe earlier?

Were the Titans actually real? And if they were, as they seemed to be, how had they come to be underneath the city?

My family knew me to be a kook. I wondered if they would believe me if I told them about this.

I backed away as the Titans clashed with each other, trying to tear each other apart as people looked on from the bleachers.

This city apparently held more secrets than I could've ever known.

CHAPTER 9

TITANIA

The first step out of the apartment upon James leaving felt different. I couldn't say why. Maybe it was the faintest hint of a cooler temperature that hung around me, caressing my skin. I inhaled deeply, longing for a greater taste of autumn. Hopefully it would be just a few days, and he'd be back. Maybe we could take things easy. Enjoy life a little. Not have to worry so much. Or maybe I was letting the seasonal wistfulness get to me.

The few hours of sleep I'd gotten after they left took the edge off the sleep-deprived disorientation. I might still need a nap today, though…

I moved toward the elevator, hands in my hoodie pockets along with one of his letters. I removed a hand just long enough to jab the button for the way down. It lit up, and I watched as the ticker above the top moved down to our floor.

When the doors began to open, I stepped forward on instinct and nearly ran Greg into the back of the elevator.

"Oh, I'm so sorry, Greg! I guess I'm a little preoccupied."

But instead of his normal, zany self, Greg's eyes were wild and frantic as I stepped beside him. He didn't even acknowledge what I had said. Instead, he glared at the *Close Door* button on the elevator, mashing it with such intensity that I was afraid it might malfunction and trap us in here.

"Are you okay?" I asked him as the doors shut and we began descending. His usual chatter still hadn't begun, and he looked like he'd seen a ghost.

"My sister's house." He stared at me, his eyes vacant. "It's on fire."

"Oh no!" I gasped. "Where does she live?"

He twitched and moved from one foot to the next as he spoke. "She lives on the outskirts of town."

I hadn't explored much of the city, so I wasn't sure what houses there were, but as the elevator doors opened and he rushed out, I spoke without thinking.

"Let me come with you; maybe I can help."

I didn't know *how* I could help. Maybe just provide moral support? Or help throw some buckets of water at it? We'd figure it out. Surely there would be people there, helping already.

He nodded, motioning for me to follow him. It briefly occurred to me that Greg was practically a stranger and I maybe shouldn't just follow him without telling someone…but this was Greg. He was harmless.

I followed him as he ran. He was fast, given his age. He seemed a little surprised I could keep up with him, and for a moment reverted to his old self, asking me inane questions about workout routines and things of that nature. But as quickly as it came, that version of him left again and his face was stony. Buildings passed by us in a blur.

"Who all lives in the house?" I asked as a pillar of smoke became evident the closer we got.

"My sister, her husband, and my niece." His reply was curt, surely in part due to how short of breath he was.

My pulse quickened at the mention of his niece. I wondered how old she was, and the closer we got the further my heart dropped.

The house was engulfed in flames. There were people standing at nearby houses, watering hoses soaking their properties in what I guessed was an attempt to stop the fire from spreading. Flames reached into the sky and moved as though tugged this way and that by invisible strings. A woman rushed up to Greg, tears cutting down her cheeks. This had to be his sister.

Her words were almost indecipherable through the hysterics. I caught that her husband was at work, so that was one person out of the way.

"She's still inside! I couldn't find her!" the woman wailed. Greg stormed toward the home, and I ran ahead of him.

Two men started running to block me, but I ducked and dodged the both of them. I looked back just in time to see them grab Greg by the arms, and he let out an unearthly growl.

I barely had time to consider the consequences of what I was about to do. All I knew was that I couldn't leave a child inside a burning home.

I took a huge gulp of clean air and slipped inside the fiery blaze, beginning my transformation immediately. A piercing scream filled the air as I disappeared from view.

I began my search as black, cracked rock with rivulets of flowing lava replaced my tan, olive skin. I took care to keep the temperature low so as not to burn straight through my clothes, though I wouldn't be able to preserve them if I had to step directly into one of the tongues of fire that now surrounded me. My hair popped with sparks as it lit up.

To my surprise, it didn't feel any hotter in the house than my normal transformation did. Perks of being a firebird, I guessed.

I moved easily through the flames that consumed the building around me. They hadn't done enough structural damage to bring the whole thing down, but that was only a matter of time, a fact I was keenly aware of as I threw open every door and cabinet I could find.

"Hello!" I called out. "Is anyone in here?"

The smoke that seemed to rise from every surface didn't impact my lungs the way it would have for a normal human. I felt a bit of scratchiness and a decreased ability to breathe, but I could sustain myself just as well as the fire could under the conditions.

I rounded a corner and found a wide staircase. I took the stairs several at a time, but on the third impact, they caved in. I instantly grew my feathered wings, regained my ground with a flap, and began ascending that way. If the little girl saw them, I could blame it on her smoke inhalation. That caused hallucinations, right?

"Hello?" I called again, louder this time.

I heard a faint sob, and my heart tried to leap out of my chest.

"If you can hear me, make a lot of noise!" I screamed into the smoke and flames.

The fire was spreading on this floor, too, belching more soot and ash into the air. I could barely see where I was going.

I followed the sound of a small hand pounding on something until I stopped at a point in the wall. I felt along the surface until a small ridge popped up, and I clawed and yanked at it until it gave way. Inside was a small attic. It looked like maybe a storage area, perhaps for family heirlooms and important papers. Two little eyes looked straight at me. The girl sat, crying and bathed in sweat, surrounded by speedily melting crayons.

I reached out to pick her up, then realized that if I did that, I would burn her. She was frozen in place, surely terrified of both the fire and me. I yanked off my hoodie, leaving my white T-shirt underneath, and threw the garment over the girl. It covered her completely. I knew from experience that hoodies were a little more fire-resistant than most everything else, at least when it came to *my* fire.

"Hold on," I murmured as I lifted her, grateful for the barrier the hoodie provided, and searched for a way out. I could hear the roof groan, threatening to collapse, and even though I could handle the fire, the girl's tender skin would be seared by it. Not to mention, I could still get knocked out by falling debris.

The most conspicuous thing would be to go straight up through the weakened roof. But going back down would risk it caving in on us. I searched for a window to the outside. Jumping from the second story was plausibly survivable. More so with my wings.

The girl's little body shook as she coughed from within the hoodie. If I ran down a hall long enough, I could break through the wall. I had more than a little added strength thanks to my spliced DNA.

The roof gave another louder, and more insistent, groan. That settled it: through a wall it was.

I ran past columns of smoke and fire, feeling the floor start to give way. My wings took both of our weight. Every muscle in my body tensed as I prepared for impact. I crashed through the wall of the house with my side, careful to shield the little girl as debris flew out. I had no idea what direction we were going or where the most bystanders would be, but I caught the wind in my wings and lowered us as best as I could before collapsing onto the ground with her on top of me. I quickly pulled the hoodie off her as she coughed and sputtered. I retracted my wings and calmed my skin as fast as I could.

A voice from behind us startled me.

"Meg?" Greg called to the little girl.

Had he seen my wings? I quickly stood, pulling my hoodie over my head to try to cover as much of my body and not-so-white-anymore shirt as possible, so he wouldn't see that my skin was fine despite having walked through fire.

He came and scooped up his niece, cradling her in his arms.

"What do you have?" he asked her as he inspected her hand, it was held tightly shut.

She opened it up wordlessly, and a piece of crumpled paper popped out and fell to the ground. I bent down to pick it up, unfolding it. She must have been drawing on it with the crayons, though I wasn't sure she was supposed to be. It looked like it had been an important document…

I froze, locking eyes with the symbol at the top of the page. A T-shaped, deconstructed DNA helix with a rounded top.

The symbol of the Titan program.

CHAPTER 10

LUNA

"We have to get out of here," I whispered to Silen when the young man walked out of the room.

"'*Have to*' seems so dramatic. I don't think this is a matter of life and death…at least, not for me," Silen countered.

If I was the sort of person to bite my tongue, mine would've been bleeding. He was insufferable!

"I can change that," I said sweetly.

He gulped.

As he should.

"What do you propose?" he asked, eyeing me cautiously.

I looked around the room. The only exit was the door, and they'd surely notice *that* opening. Whatever game they were playing, they seemed far more competent than most government employees I'd met. We'd have to have a solid plan, and a quick execution of it.

There was a wall clock, but that seemed pretty useless. Unless…

"Hey, do you think you can make an explosion with a clock?" I tossed the idea to Silen.

He furrowed his eyebrows. "I'm a scientist, not a pyromaniac!"

"Okay," I said as I shushed him. "I was just asking."

I sighed, craning my neck back to stare at the ceiling.

Getting Silen free would be no big deal; I could just shift my head to wolf and gnaw through his restraints. Perhaps I could scoot my chair over to him to untie mine before I did that. Otherwise, he might up and leave without me. But I didn't want to let him know that part of the plan until I knew how we could escape this room.

I banged the back of my head against the chair, which scooted it closer and closer to the wall behind me.

Think. Think. Think.

A bit of dust from the ceiling came down and landed in my eye.

"Ahhhh," I hissed as I tried to blink it out. I couldn't rub it with my hands tied. I considered that this might be more torturous than if they had waterboarded us.

Once the debris cleared out of my eye, I saw Silen smirking in amusement. I gave him a glare first, then directed it at the ceiling.

My expression loosened as I saw a ceiling title just slightly out of place.

"That's it," I whispered.

Silen looked at me like I'd lost my mind, which was rich coming from him.

"The tiles." I jutted my chin upward to direct his attention. "We can move them, climb up there, and escape through the venting."

I was quite proud of his nod of approval.

"But how do we get out of the restraints?" He wiggled his hands behind his back, which shook his arms and shoulders.

I debriefed him on my plan for that and, as I expected, he was hesitant to untie me first. But he was equally, if not more, scared of me just going wolf and attacking him right here and now. So he reluctantly obliged. I scooted the chair around until the back of mine was up against the back of his and, after a moment of blind searching, he found the ropes on my wrists.

"What if they catch us?" he asked anxiously as he worked at the knots.

"Then I'll bite them," I said, matter-of-factly.

The answer was always biting.

I couldn't see his face, so I didn't know how he reacted to that, but he kept working on the knots until I felt them loosening. I anxiously pulled as the tightness released. My wrists slipped out, and I sat for just a second to admire the sight of my untethered hands.

"Hurry up," Silen hissed anxiously.

I changed my head into the head of a wolf, my nose elongating into a snout. Teeth lengthening and sharpening. Silen twitched anxiously in anticipation of me cutting him loose. It was efficient, biting the restraints. All it took was one deft chomp with the side of my mouth, and they fell to the floor.

"Ouch!" Silen cried, holding up his hands.

A small bit of blood pooled out of a scratch. Collateral damage.

"You'll live," I assured him when my face was human once more.

I took one of the chairs and shoved it toward the door, doing my best to wedge it in such a way that it might stop or delay an entry.

I shoved Silen toward the already ajar ceiling tile, dragging his chair behind us.

I could make him go first, but I wasn't confident he'd be able to find his way. I wondered if there was some sort of piping, or if it was more of an attic crawl space that we'd find up there. Either way, we needed to move quickly.

Yanking the chair into position, I climbed onto it. I tried to reach for the ceiling tile, but I was too short.

"Boost me," I commanded Silen.

He looked incredulous. Anything that wasn't beakers and brainiac science was beneath him.

"Just do it!" I hissed.

He stepped forward, moving to allow me to crawl onto his back and use it as a launch pad. My fingers gripped the lip of the tile, knocking it further out of place and giving me space to move up. I hoisted myself, catching my abdomen halfway across the sturdy piece of metal that held the tiles in place. I pushed farther up and past the pain, clawing my way through and into the insulation-filled crawl space. I turned around, gingerly lying on my belly to distribute my weight across the beams, and reached down for Silen.

"It's a lot roomier than I thought would be," I coaxed, seeing his trepidation.

He stood in the chair, anxiety clear on his face. I didn't know if he thought he was going to get caught before he could get up, or if he didn't like enclosed spaces. It was hard to tell with him.

He seemed very vain. Maybe it was just that he thought there'd be germs involved.

Silen reached up, fingertips just shy of the lip of the beam holding the tiles. I reached my arms down, hooking my shoes to a different beam so that he wouldn't drag me down. He gripped my forearms and I flexed my feet and legs as his weight pulled at me, threatening to send me flying forward. I dragged him up, slowly slithering backward until he could grasp enough on his own to stabilize himself.

As soon as he wriggled fully past the opening, I took the ceiling tile and replaced it in its original position. There was nothing I could do about the dust and insulation that had dropped onto the floor and chair during the operation, but it wouldn't matter as long as we were gone by the time they noticed.

CHAPTER 11

TITANIA

The world felt like it was spinning out. The smell of smoke was suddenly overpowering and nauseating. My breathing was erratic, but at least I had the excuse of having been in a burning building. I struggled to orient myself.

Greg was telling his niece something, but I couldn't catch what. Firemen in bulky gear and hats blurred in and out of my vision as they rushed to check on the girl.

One came toward me, but for the life of me I couldn't understand a word he said. My ears rang so loud, I realized I couldn't hear anything but the ringing.

My mind was elsewhere. I struggled to make sense of what I'd just seen on the piece of paper the little girl had. It looked identical to the logo on the computer in the underwater facility we'd just visited. The same logo haunted my dreams from my time with Silen when I'd been genetically altered in the first place.

I hadn't seen it right. Surely, I hadn't seen it right. We were safe here. There was no one working on the Titan project here.

"I think…shock." Greg's words were warped, but I could tell he was looking at me.

A fireman grabbed my arm, alongside Greg, and dragged me away from the house. It crumbled behind us, collapsing under the strain of the supports being burned away. The wave of heat and sound didn't even startle me, which I think worried them more.

"What's your name?" The fireman's voice was clear now, but time seemed to move like sludge.

Did I want to give him my name? No. I didn't think I wanted this getting back to Cassandra. I was clear-headed enough to know that. She'd kinda wanted us to keep a low profile, after all. That was part of the deal. I opened my mouth to lie to him.

"Titania," Greg answered for me. I winced.

"I need her to answer the questions, to make sure she's okay," the fireman explained to Greg, concern painted on his face after my wince.

"Oh, sorry!" he said innocently, and I knew he meant well. He was just a little oblivious. It was part of his charm.

"Are you hurt?" The fireman turned back to me, moving my arms and legs a tiny bit to see if I complained.

The fireman wanted to poke and prod me. I let him until I heard someone behind him say that he wanted to take me and Meg to the hospital to be checked out.

"I'm fine," I insisted.

"That would be a miracle," the fireman said, in a very direct manner, "You ran into a burning building with no mask, no protection, and apparently fell a floor."

"Miracles happen every day, you know?" I said. What else was there to say?

I squirmed away from him. He tried to insist I go with him, but there wasn't much he could really do.

"I've got somewhere I need to be," I said, catching sight of some onlookers headed our way. The fewer people who saw my face, the better.

I pulled up my hood and quickly walked away from the disaster. Past all the cute houses and gawking onlookers. I could feel the heat radiating off the remains of the house now that I was fully human again and had a bit of distance from other people. I felt bad for the family. Even though all of them made it out, losing a home was a big deal.

I would know…this wasn't the first time I'd fled a burning building myself.

I was nearly a block down the road when something tapped my shoulder.

I turned, ready for anything. But all that stood before me was Greg, his usual demeanor having fallen by the wayside.

"Titania," he said, tripping over his words. "I-I…I just want to thank you."

I blushed, flustered. How was a person supposed to interact with Greg when he wasn't being eccentric?

"You're welcome," I said, waving my hands awkwardly as I tried to brush it off. "It was no big deal. I'm glad she's okay."

Greg's eyes lingered on mine for much longer than I felt comfortable with. It was like he was looking for something. I shifted nervously.

"I really have to go; I have somewhere I need to be," I insisted. It felt rude, but I couldn't stay here a second longer. I needed to be far away from this. From what happened.

"Okay." Greg nodded, swallowing hard. "Please do go in if you feel sick. I don't know how you…did that."

His eyes were unfocused. Perhaps he was in shock, too. He looked like he was contemplating life, the universe, *everything* in that moment.

"I will," I promised.

As I walked away, I made a promise to myself—no more stunts like this. That was too close. Way too close.

CHAPTER 12

JAMES

When we didn't have the girls with us worrying about going too fast, the ATCV could fly. I had to admit, it was nice to go on a trip with Adam and Trevor—just us guys. When the girls were with us, we couldn't help but worry about their safety. This way we could be a little more…reckless.

Adam revved it up and pushed it further and further to see just how fast it would go. Trevor and I were both white-knuckled, but in the best way possible. It was good for us to get the adrenaline going; we'd need it to break Luna and Silen free from their captors.

Trevor tapped Adam on the shoulder as the landscape flew by in a flash. Adam slowed down enough that the wind wouldn't overpower what Trevor wanted to say.

"I gotta take a leak, man. Can we stop?" Trevor asked Adam.

We both knew Adam didn't want to stop. He wanted Luna back yesterday. But we'd been driving for five hours. To be honest, I needed to take a leak, too.

Adam took it well. He stopped the ATCV near the edge of the woods and parked it so we could hop off. Trevor and I went off in separate directions, did our business, and returned.

"Do you need to go, too?" I offered Adam.

"That'd probably be a good idea," he acknowledged, somewhat reluctantly.

He left the tracker on the seat of the ATCV. I watched it blink while he was gone. It was a low, consistent rhythm that was hypnotizing to watch. Trevor picked it up and studied it, too.

"We're getting real close," he declared. There was a hint of trepidation in his voice. "I can't believe Luna got kidnapped. I never thought I'd see the day."

"She does seem pretty resourceful and sharp," I agreed.

It really was odd that she'd gotten kidnapped. She was scrappy. I was ready to fight, and ready to hear all about how they ended up kidnapped in the first place—my money was on Silen—and ready to get home to Titania.

Titania.

My cheeks flushed as I remembered the letters I'd left to her. She'd surely read a few by now. Maybe I could make a pact with her that we just wouldn't talk about them. She might not agree to it, but a man could try. I could just distract her any time she brought it up. She was easily distractible, right? The whole thing was so embarrassing!

Adam lumbered back, snapping twigs on the ground as he went.

"Ready, gentlemen?" he asked, picking the tracker back up. He studied it for a moment, then stuck it in his pocket.

We both nodded, hopping back on the ATCV behind him. We were barely ready when he took off, accelerating the machine as fast as it would let him. Somehow, we both managed to stay on.

It was easy to get stiff riding on the thing for so long. Having gotten a chance to get off and walk around had only made that more clear upon returning to it. My neck felt rigid; I moved it around trying to loosen it up just as Adam slammed on the brakes, almost shaking Trevor and me loose again. My head whipped around, making me dizzy for a moment. The pills for radiation poisoning had worked, but I still felt prone to dizziness and nausea.

"What? What happened?" Trevor demanded.

Adam swung his leg off the ATCV and pulled the tracker out of his pocket. He walked away from the vehicle and toward a small lake to our right. Trevor and I exchanged confused glances as he reeled his arm back and threw the tracker into the water at full force.

Trevor's mouth was agape as Adam remounted the ATCV.

"What'd you do that for?"

"They were always going to have the advantage in this situation. It's their turf, their tracker, their demands. This is one less advantage they have. We're close enough that I can find the way from here, and it'll give us just a bit of leeway from when they expect us to when we'll actually arrive. They'll think we're taking a break." He motioned to the lake. "Right here."

That was smart, I thought. A small advantage was better than no advantage at all.

"We should be there in the next thirty minutes," Adam said, revving the engine back up. He took off so fast that Trevor and I had to once again cling on for dear life. Once the initial shock was over from almost falling off for the third time in mere minutes, we laughed at the ridiculousness of it all.

Soon. We'd be there soon. And Adam would be a little less neurotic again with Luna by his side.

CHAPTER 13

MELODY

I was getting better at maneuvering the brakes on my wheelchair. Which was good, because I didn't want to run over any little fingers or toes. It was far superior to being confined in a fish tank. I really had thought I was going to freeze to death in that tank. I felt a little exhausted from all the changes and flurry of activity.

Since Adam, Luna, Titania, and James had rescued me, life had been a whirlwind. It was easy to feel overwhelmed when the only thing that had happened before was waiting for death. Every day now was a little easier.

The gym was bustling with movement, kids and kid-critters running this way and that, screaming their heads off.

Jen, the lady who took care of all the Titan kids, seemed a little low on energy. I couldn't blame her, especially since she usually ran all of this herself. I was happy to be able to help her. It was easy to feel useless when you were sporting a fish tail and less mobile than everyone else. On land, at least.

The kids all loved me, and the feeling was mutual. Especially the skunk. He would sit on my lap and want to zoom across the gym in my wheelchair.

"My turn!" He reached for me to pick him up. I lifted him and mentally made a note to ask Adam to install a seatbelt when he got back. I hoped he'd be back soon. There was more I wanted to talk to him about. A lot more. We'd not gotten much time at all, except on the trip home from the underwater compound. He was different than the others…and I had more questions. I had things I wanted to tell them, but I didn't know if he wanted me to just tell *him*, or if it was okay to tell everyone. There was so much I witnessed and heard that was contextless to me, but valuable to them. Who knew spying and eavesdropping could be a useful skill! I didn't know what the others knew about what Adam knew. He seemed pretty secretive overall.

The child in my arms squealed as we rushed across the room. I started braking early so he didn't fly into the wall, using my left arm as a seat belt. Jen came in at that exact moment.

She laughed. "Having fun?" she teased, scooping up the skunk boy who begged to go again. I nodded. "I'm glad you have the energy for this." Jen gestured to the whole building.

I smiled back. This was a lot better than being trapped in a tank.

"I'm just glad I don't scare them." I gestured to my tail.

"I don't think anything could." Jen laughed, ruffling the skunk boy's hair. "They are pretty scary all on their own."

CHAPTER 14

LUNA

"Don't step on the tiles, keep to the metal bars," I whispered to Silen. He glared in my general direction, like I should assume he knew that. But I couldn't assume anything when it came to him. He was one of those people who was so smart he was stupid.

"It's pitch black in here," he whined.

"Just because they can't see us, doesn't mean they can't hear us. Keep quiet!" I rolled my eyes at him.

I scoped out the path before us, what was visible anyway. There was really no light, but I'd had a few more moments to adjust than he had. I could tell some areas were smaller than others. I really didn't want to be crawling on my hands and knees up here.

I changed my eyes to wolf eyes so I could see better and decide which way we should go. One direction was a dead end, and it went up against the wall—I *guessed* it was a wall—of the attic or ceiling. Maybe that meant that was the side of the building, too. The question was whether it was the back of the building, the side, or the front. I doubted highly that it was the front; it wouldn't make sense to keep prisoners near an exit.

Silen shuffled around behind me in the dark, which made the hair on the back of my neck stand on end.

I wanted to get a move on. We could've gone to the right, but I thought going straight was the best idea.

"This way." I surged ahead, stepping on the areas where the metal connected for more support.

He followed behind me, albeit less gracefully since he didn't have night vision. We came upon a narrowing area where we had to crouch down. I groaned, planting my knees against the metal corners.

"How about I go first?" Silen suggested, "My eyes have adjusted now."

I let him crawl ahead of me, leaning out of the way so he could enter the passageway. At least I wouldn't have the creeps from him being behind me. This way I could keep an eye on him, in case he pulled any stunts.

Wherever we were, I could hear the sound of people talking below us. I tried to listen as we carefully moved through the small space.

The sound of James' name stopped me in my tracks. It was that guy, the one who seemed to be running things here. He was talking about James. I stopped to try and hear more, which made Silen impatient. He turned back to look at me, scraping the side of the wall. It sent a cloud of dust into the air.

My eyes went wide as I watched the puff descend upon us. Was Silen allergic to dust? Did people only sneeze when they were allergic to it, or from it getting in their nose at all?

I shook my head, unsure if he could see me.

He pressed forward, and I breathed a sigh of relief. A premature one.

The tickle buried itself inside my nose. I tried to suppress it, my eyes watering profusely at the effort.

I had it under control, balancing myself on my legs and one arm as I held my nose shut with my right hand. Silen's shoe caught one of the tiles, displacing it and breaking my concentration. I sneezed.

Suddenly everything was eerily silent.

No no no no *no*!

Silen took off, not even trying to hide the noise. I tried to scramble after him, but the tile he moved tripped me up, and one of my legs fell through. He disappeared into the darkness and ignored my hissed calls of his name. This was the thanks I got for helping him escape? I should've left him in that office!

I tried to heave my leg back up, but my arm slipped and punched a hole right through one of the ceiling tiles. The more I struggled, the worse the situation became. I was caught at an odd angle between my arm and leg, and I couldn't get enough leverage to get myself out of it.

A strong grip wrapped itself around my ankle.

I was toast.

CHAPTER 15

TITANIA

My lungs felt strange. The chill in the air interacted a little differently with them after the fire. It was sharper somehow, the sensation of breathing it in and out. Maybe I was just a little more sensitive to any input after the day I'd had.

I felt around in my pocket for the letter. James' letter. I wished I could have read the ones he had burned, but I'd settle for any piece of him he'd let me see. This little dance we did, around each other and around our feelings, seemed to be a one step forward, two steps back proposition. What could we expect, being two orphans? It was understandable that we both had some attachment issues. That's where all of our pacts to never leave each other as children came from. If we had each other, we had everything we needed.

I was grateful he was trusting me with these while he was gone.

He'd given me directions to his favorite place in the woods. It was the perfect distance from the city, an edge of it I'd never explored. As I entered the area, I saw how it could remind him of me. It was like the woods near the compound that we'd grown up in. The ones we'd played chase in and spent the few truly free moments of childhood in.

The smell of dirt and musty leaves greeted me as I stepped into a world that was much quieter and simpler than the one I lived in.

I stepped lightly around a ring of mushrooms, careful not to crush any of them. They had grown in a cute little fairy circle near a downed log.

It was inviting, the perfect place to sit and read. I could turn around and not see a hint of civilization anymore. If only we could run away and all live in these woods. No government, no secrets, no fears. Just us. If it was just us, that might work. But it wasn't. We had Luna, and Adam, and Trevor, and Miranda, and Natalie, and Jen, and now Melody, and all of the children to care for. We all needed each other. Still, a part of my soul yearned to run away with James and leave all this behind. Never speak of it again. Drop off the map, fake our own deaths or something. Would I ever be able to convincingly die as a phoenix, though? Would people always be waiting a year for me to resurrect? Maybe it would work if I seemed to die as a human. We didn't actually know what would happen under that circumstance.

I shook the thoughts away, shaking my body to expel them involuntarily. I surprised myself with how my mind wandered. I needed to live in reality. And maybe take a vacation.

I pulled out the letter from my hoodie pocket. The smell of smoke wafted off of it. I found myself getting upset over that, but I reminded myself that it was still readable, unlike the ones James had burnt. This one easily could've met the same fiery fate if it had fallen out in the house. But it just had character now.

I unfolded it, my heart skipping a beat at the sight of James' handwriting. I felt a little silly, but there was something about reading a note, something written just for you, from someone you love. Even if it was a letter written to a dead person.

Dear Titania,

I went for a walk (well, a run) with your ghost today. She runs through the woods, just like you used to. I can almost hear you laughing sometimes. I think the others would think I'm crazy if they knew. They worry already. I don't blame them. It makes me angry, though, like it's my fault for making them worry. But it's nothing I can help. I just need space.

No, I need you.

I run after her, your ghost. I know...stupid, right? But it makes me feel better. I never catch her, just like I never caught you. Maybe if I was just a little faster, I could've saved you.

I miss you.

I love you.

James

I read, and reread, and when I came back to myself, I had tears leaking into the creases of my smile.

CHAPTER 16

THE LITTLE GIRL

The little girl dutifully traveled behind the adults down the dark hallway. The chill of the shadows reached out to her, grasping at her exposed skin. She wasn't sure about this. She wasn't sure about the people she was with. Not after she'd slipped going down the stairs.

They were wet to the touch. Slimy. It made her shiver. She let go to wipe her hands. The adults caught her as she fell, but their grumbling hurt her feelings. It had been an impulsive instinct, not something she'd meant to do.

She'd been with them only a few days and had started coming out of her shell in a way she hadn't before. A choice that she was now wondering if she would regret.

She had far more freedom here than she'd experienced before. She hadn't been able to see and do nearly as much when she was in the orphanage or in the strange man's house. The little girl had come to learn that she loved walking outside in the sun. This was something else entirely.

Even the floor seemed slimy to her, though she couldn't feel it through her shoes to be sure. She was grateful she had shoes on.

One of the men seemed to feel that she wasn't walking fast enough. He hooked his arm under hers and started dragging her forward. She whined, but of course, he couldn't hear it. Nobody could ever hear it. She considered going limp, but she knew where that had led before. Anger and beatings.

Where could they be going, she wondered. She could see that the tunnel extended far beyond a bridge that crossed over to the other side. They made their way to it, turning to cross. She craned her head to see down the long tunnel but couldn't make out the end of it. Something about it called to her. Maybe it was a sense of adventure, maybe it was an escape. Whatever it was, she couldn't follow it. She was led forward, nothing more than a prisoner. For as long as she wasn't free to dictate where her footprints landed, she was property of whoever did make that decision.

CHAPTER 17

LUNA

Silen was long gone when the person holding my ankle managed to drag me down through the tiles, despite my kicking. The person had an iron grip on me! As I crashed down, I was caught by the boy who had kidnapped us and also by his boss. It was the boss' right hand that had wrapped around my leg.

My shoulders hurt, and my legs, and…well, everything.

"Where is the guy?" the kidnapper asked his boss as he handed me off.

"Send out an alert," the boss said, gripping my wrist now as he looked up at the ceiling. "Tell everyone to start looking!"

His lackey rushed off to accomplish the task.

When he was out of sight, the boss looked at me, studying my face with such intensity that I had to look away.

"You're very resourceful. That was impressive, Luna," he said.

How did he know my name? An unsettling feeling washed over me. Who was this guy?

I jerked my wrist, trying to get out of his grasp. It hurt to even try. He smiled as he watched my eyes shift to the hand holding my wrist.

At the top of his wrist I saw a flash of something silver. Metal?

He watched me as I tried to make sense of what was happening. I wasn't weak; I could hold my own in any fight I'd ever been in, tranquilizers notwithstanding. Those were cheating. How was he hanging onto me?

He held his arm up at an angle, letting the long sleeves he was wearing droop down to expose his wrist. Where flesh should've been was smooth, shiny metal. He took a step toward me, a sympathetic but amused look on his face.

I looked him in the eye, forcing defiance into my expression.

"You're not the only experiment in the world, miss."

CHAPTER 18

JAMES

Adam practically threw the ATCV into the bushes when we came near to the location that he was sure the tracker had been leading to. He was strong, I just hadn't realized how strong. His whole body was buzzing with nervous energy. Trevor and I had to dismount quickly to avoid being thrown into the bushes, too.

This didn't look like a Lumis facility. It lacked the bland white brick paint, cage covering the backyard, and general distaste for windows. This was something else. It made me uneasy. We knew the score with the Lumis facilities. Was it possible that this was some completely different enemy?

We followed Adam's hulking form as he lumbered toward the front door. Were we going to just barge in? We weren't going to be stealthy? Sneak through a window or back door? Come up with a plan?

I shot Trevor a panicked glance as Adam knocked twice on the front door. What was he doing?! It wasn't like we could even claim to be traveling salesmen or something; that was something of the old world that didn't exist anymore! We weren't even in government clothing where we could pass as being on official business.

My heart leapt out of my chest as Adam took hold of the door and ripped it straight off its hinges. Trevor's eyes went wide as he stood beside me. A young man stood behind the door, mouth agape as his hand hovered where the knob had been seconds before.

Adam reeled back and punched the poor kid straight in the face, sending him flying backward.

"WHERE IS SHE!" Adam's voice boomed, like he had used a megaphone. Trevor's hands flew to his ears.

Adam's whole body was turning red from rage. Teenaged faces peeked out from doors leading who knows where as we entered the building, only to retreat and slam the doors shut instantly upon seeing the look on Adam's face. His eyes were wild. He looked inhuman, and it sent a cold chill through my body.

He punched holes in the closed doors, splintering the wood. He bent to look through them, checking every one for Luna, with people cowering in abject terror inside. Most were shaking, and I honestly couldn't blame them. One woman screamed and fainted, a man behind her caught her as she slunk to the ground.

A door at the end of the hall opened, and I flinched as I tried to anticipate what would happen next. A man stepped out, a woman with him.

Adam stampeded toward them, with Trevor and I running behind him in an attempt to keep up. As soon as I saw the lock of blonde hair with gray splashed in it, I knew we'd found Luna. But who was that with her? He didn't look like Silen...

Adam made contact with the guy hanging onto Luna. And by *made contact*, I mean he hit him and sent that dude flying into the wall. Adam shook his fist, then gripped Luna for a split second as she rushed behind him, worry painted on her face. Why was she worried? That wasn't like her. She could scare the pants off of anything! Was she worried that Adam was gonna kill her captor?

The man's eyes fluttered, and he rose from the crater in the wall. I was a bit surprised that he got up from that; it was a pretty hard hit.

Adam cocked back for another, but when he let loose with a right hook, the man blocked his fist with his own right arm. Luna wedged between Trevor and me, her eyes wide.

"I don't want to fight," the man said. "I just want to talk."

"Stealing women isn't the best way to initiate conversation," Adam growled, sending an uppercut into the man's unprotected stomach with his left arm.

The man doubled over, clearly impacted by the hit. Adam turned back for a second to check on Luna. I'd never seen the look he gave her on anyone before. Their bond was something else.

The man looked up at us, and his eyes went from frustration to recognition.

"James?" he said, his voice slightly strained.

I cocked my head. How did he know my name? Was he the one who requested me?

I walked toward him, surging some of the lion DNA into circulation in case this ended in a fight.

But he didn't look like he wanted to fight anyone. He looked like the wind had gotten knocked out of him. And it didn't seem like it was from the punch.

"James…it's…" He searched my face. "It's Brandon."

CHAPTER 19

TITANIA

"You've been busy," Cassandra said, setting down a cup she'd just taken a drink from. The wrinkles around her mouth harbored a tiny bit of the liquid. From the hint of an attitude she already possessed, I wondered what was in it.

Her voice carried a false sense of ambivalence, but the implicit sense of disturbance hung in the air.

Cassandra's blonde bob and big purple eyes were deceptively soft and sweet for her true personality.

My pulse quickened. I knew it was too much to hope that she wouldn't find out about the house fire.

I stuffed down my instinct to start talking. To compulsively say that I could explain. Instead, I gathered every ounce of composure I possessed and looked her straight in the eye.

"No more than usual." I accompanied it with a little laugh. "But yeah, kids do keep you busy under the most normal of circumstances."

I had been helping Jen. That wasn't a lie. Had she heard what had happened to Luna? Maybe that's what this was about.

Something flashed in her eyes. Anger? Annoyance? Irritation?

"I understand that you and your neighbor, Greg, are quite close…"

I groaned inwardly.

Of course. This had to be about the fire. Greg probably couldn't keep it quiet. But why wasn't she just coming out with it? Yelling at me and telling me to lay lower next time.

"I don't know…he's just my neighbor," I said truthfully.

I casually looked around at her office decorations, trying to get away from her accusatory gaze. Her taste seemed to be a mix of the old and the new. She had a globe, the kind from before everything collapsed, but next to that was a framed map that showed the world with updated boundaries. Additional frames behind her desk contained awards and recognition she had received during her time as mayor, as well as some from before. Most of them seemed to have been awarded by the Haven Club, Reunion City's prestigious and exclusive society, and boasted its logo in glittering gold ink.

Cassandra's desk itself was tidy, with a holder for pens and several organizers for papers. In the corner of it, she had a snake statue. I could feel the fangs from the past, and I shivered to keep myself in the present. What a weird thing to decorate with.

"Oh really?" Cassandra's eyebrows looked like they were on their way to Mars. "My neighbors don't risk their lives in a house fire for me."

It couldn't be because of her *shining* personality, I thought sarcastically.

"I couldn't let somebody die."

"Noble, truly." Cassandra took another swig of whatever was in her cup again. "Is that the only reason you entered that house?"

I was starting to feel exasperated, and I was sure it showed on my face. What other reason would there be?

"Nah, I did it because I was bored."

I knew I shouldn't have said it. My sarcasm got me in trouble even when James and I were at Lone Leaf, the compound we'd grown up in together.

Her face turned red, then her ears.

"This isn't funny!" she hissed, slamming her hand on the table.

I flinched—even though I wasn't surprised—just to appease her. I didn't need a Cassandra meltdown.

"I'm sorry, I didn't realize saving little girls was off the list of approved activities," I said, but with no malice in my voice.

"Did you take anything?" she growled.

"Besides the little girl?" I crossed my arms. "No."

"Don't lie to me," she warned.

"What would I even take? It was a BURNING HOUSE! I wasn't about to stop and rob them blind. Seriously, why would you think that?"

Without James here to mediate, I wasn't particularly inclined to placate her. This was ridiculous!

"You better be telling me the truth. The future of you and your little friends here in Reunion City is on the line here."

"Is that a threat?" My jaw was on the floor. "If it's that much of a problem, I won't save any more children from burning buildings. I promise."

"You know that's not what this is about." She downed the rest of her drink with irritation.

"Then what is it about?"

Instead of answering my question, she tipped her chin to something in the corner. Some*one.*

A tall, buff man in black strode over and looped his hand under my arm.

I was being kicked out.

I needed to talk to Jen. I wished Luna was here. Whatever was going on, it wasn't good. And it wasn't about that little girl.

CHAPTER 20

URBAN EXPLORERS

"What do you think this was for?" the sandy-haired boy asked his companion, a ski mask covering his face.

Dust covered the floor, the chairs, the desks.

"Probably just an office park," said his redheaded companion. "People were obsessed with paperwork before."

"That's crazy." The sandy-haired boy swiped his fingers along the dust of a dark, wood desk. There was so much inside of these abandoned buildings that could be used. Why was it being left to languish? It was so wasteful.

"You're telling me. They probably thought they'd have access to all they ever wanted, forever. They didn't know that paper could be taken so easily."

"I wonder if anyone that used this office is even still alive?" The sandy-haired boy spun around, taking it all in.

The floor gave a groan, and he moved closer to his friend near the window, unsteady on his feet, not wanting to fall through. It was just a little groan. As long as he moved nice and slowly…

CRASH

The floor gave way. His ears were filled with the sound of rushing air and a scream from his friend above. It was piercing. He braced himself for the crash. They were three stories high. Would he fall all the way? Or just a floor? The hospital could patch him up, he was sure, but he'd get a hefty fine for urban exploring. There would be no good excuse for the injuries he'd sustain, and depending on how bad they were, he wouldn't even be able to deny where he'd gotten them because they'd have to pick him up here.

His mom was gonna kill him.

His back made impact with something hard, and it knocked the wind out of him. He heard a squeak, he could've sworn it. And when he tentatively opened his eyes that he had clamped shut, he saw a little mouse in the corner of the floor. The floor that he somehow wasn't lying on. He craned his neck to look up.

A woman with sharp facial features looked down on him with a disappointed glare.

He gulped.

She was strong. How had she caught him, without faltering? Who was she? She was beautiful and scary in equal measure.

"You," she said sternly, "are not where you're supposed to be."

The more cautious redheaded companion stood on the second story, peering down through the gaping hole his friend had fallen through. He looked as terrified as the boy caught by the woman felt.

"Can you stand?" the woman asked. Her eyes appraised the boy.

His voice was trapped in his throat. Could he?

He wiggled, trying to swing his feet down to see, but he was immediately off balance and swayed toward the floor. The woman steadied him, and in his peripheral vision, he saw movement off in the corner of the room.

A young woman, even younger and smaller than the one who had caught him, emerged from behind a wall in another part of the building. She stepped toward both of the boys. He tensed. Were these guards patrolling the buildings for the city? Just how much trouble were they in?

A girl in a wheelchair came in through the front door, her face pensive as she stopped short, the debris on the floor posing a problem for her. She looked to be around his age, with a blanket draped over her legs.

The younger woman looked to the boy above, and then back down.

"You guys should be careful; you never know what kind of characters are out here. It's not safe." Her voice was so small, but her eyes held empathy and concern that weighed the fallen boy down. Guilt settled into him.

"Then why are *you* here?" his friend asked from the second story.

The woman who had caught the boy shot a look at her friend. One that told them that, perhaps, these women weren't supposed to be here either.

CHAPTER 21

LUNA

I watched as a look of recognition crossed James' face.

Brandon? Our captor's name was Brandon?

LAAAAME.

The hallway was in pandemonium. People were shouting and pressing in. I couldn't get my bearings to figure out what to do. Silen was still in the ceiling, but who knew how long it would stay that way. Every second that ticked by was a second he was probably getting away. I doubted his scaredy-cat ways would keep him from taking the opportunity to get out of dodge.

Especially when Adam was providing the perfect distraction. I had only seen him lose his cool one other time, and to be honest, once was enough for a lifetime. I wanted these people to make it out alive so we could at least question them. He needed to calm down a little, but I knew there would be no convincing him of that.

Adam snarled at the people pressing in and they backed off, a little. He turned his attention back to Brandon and postured like he was going to punch him again.

James latched on, pulling and tugging at Adam with all of his might. Adam shook him off, but didn't deliver the threatened blow.

Brandon stepped half a pace back, hands up in front of him in a gesture that was both defensive and soothing. His face was contorted with an expression that I could only call confusion.

Actually, we were probably all wearing our own version of that expression. Well, except for Trevor, who had half shifted to his long green lizard form, elongating his face and obscuring his expression. But clarity could come later. For now, we needed to make sure Silen was accounted for.

"Hey!" I shouted, but everyone's attention stayed locked on one another.

"Hey!" I shouted again, trying to be heard through the gawking grunts of the mess of people that crowded the hall. They were cemented in place, by shock I assumed. It wasn't every day that you had someone break into your place of work and start sending people flying. I found myself a little sympathetic despite my absolute annoyance that they wouldn't give us more space.

"Adam!" I demanded, letting my voice become shrill. He held up a hand, urging me to wait as he continued his stare down with Brandon. He looked annoyed, and I thought to myself how much he should really just be grateful that he was still breathing.

"Silen!" I shouted at the very top of my lungs. Adam wasn't used to me being hysterical, and I knew that would get his attention. "Is. MISSING!"

Adam's head turned.

CHAPTER 22

URBAN EXPLORERS

"Do you have parents or someone we can take you to? Are you in pain at all? I can take you to the hospital," the woman holding the sandy haired-boy offered. The boys' eyes went wide. They did not want to have to explain this to their parents *or* to someone at the hospital. You could face some pretty hefty fines for urban exploring around here.

"No, no," the redheaded boy on the second story said. "We're fine. He can walk." His eyes pleaded with his companion to walk.

The sandy-haired boy took his weight off of the lady and stood, a little shaky due to the adrenaline. He was sure that the pain would set in, once that wore off.

His legs were too heavy, and he tripped as he tried to walk away. She fixed both boys with a stare that said they were not getting out of this easily.

"Let us escort you back into town. Regardless of where your final destination is, I'll sleep a little bit better tonight knowing that you made it back there safely."

She was very motherly, in the most aggressive way possible.

They were in *so* much trouble.

The younger girl tailed behind, and the sandy-haired boy waited for his friend to descend the stairs and join them.

"How'd you get into this as a hobby?" the lady who had caught him asked.

The girl in the wheelchair started backing up out of the building, making room for us to exit.

The redheaded boy looked at his friend, wondering if he would actually answer.

"There isn't much to do around here." It was the only honest reply.

"You don't like the little cinema, coffee, any of the restaurants, or any of the classes I'm sure are offered in town?"

"Those all cost money." The sandy-haired boy frowned, realizing he'd just inadvertently labeled himself and his family as poor.

"Oh, I can understand that." The lady became more reserved, pulling her jacket around her.

To the sandy-haired boy's surprise, his friend piped up.

"Plus, all the cinema ever shows is government-approved stuff. It's the same thing over and over again. Nothing's new. Nothing is exciting."

"I suppose reruns are definitely less exciting than almost breaking your neck." She winked at the both of them. The sandy-haired boy felt heat rise on the back of his neck.

"I'd just like to see more of the world, the way it was before. Nobody ever talks about it," he mumbled. He knew he sounded like an angsty teenager, but he was one, so what was the problem with that? They were all forced to act like adults when they weren't. This was supposed to be a time to take risks and do stupid things that you don't tell your parents about. For kids before, it was falling out of trees. For them, it was falling down a story of an abandoned building. They always survived!

"Your parents don't talk about it?" the younger girl asked as she flanked the side of their little group. Her breath shown in the cold air as she paced along.

"They don't like to talk about *before*," said the sandy-haired boy.

"Yeah," agreed his friend. "My dad gets really upset when it gets brought up. The only way we can even be in a place like this is because of his job with the government."

"Oh?" the older lady asked. "What does he do?"

"I don't know, something stupid," the redheaded boy answered. "Something with broadcasting. So I guess he gets to randomly scare people for a living."

"That's one way to look at it." The lady chuckled.

"You won't tell him, will you?" The redheaded boy suddenly remembered the predicament they were in. His dad could get in a little bit of trouble for them exploring like this.

The lady looked thoughtful for a moment, glancing at both boys.

"How about this," she said as they walked. "I won't tell anyone I saw you, if you don't tell anyone you saw me. Deal?"

CHAPTER 23

THE LITTLE GIRL

The little girl looked so out of place in the middle of the dome-shaped room. Empty seats lined the walls in almost every direction. She looked around, taking it all in. Sitting cross-legged in the center of a roped off ring, she had a clear vantage point of nearly everything. Two adults, a woman and a man, stood off to the side talking. It seemed like all they ever did was talk, but they only ever talked to her to talk down to her. She tried to talk to them, but even here, nobody seemed to hear or understand her. It made her want to scream! Regardless, she knew nobody would hear it.

They talked and talked, and she realized that they weren't paying any attention to her at all. She started crawling over to the edge of the ring and slid right through the bottom space underneath one of the stretchy pieces of fencing that enclosed it. When she hit the floor, she paused. Waiting. Watching to see if they had heard her or noticed. But nobody came around to get her.

Her heartbeat picked up as she began exploring. She was so used to being monitored all of the time. What to explore first, she wondered. Off to the far end of the dome-shaped room was a dark corner. She squinted. She wasn't sure, but she thought that there might be a door.

A door could lead out.

With a single glance back, she found that they were still just chatting away without noticing her absence at all.

She made quick work of crossing the room, her curiosity growing by the second. Would she be free? What would she do if she was? She would figure it out. Her heart leapt at the possibility. The little girl almost tripped from going too fast in her excitement.

The talking got dimmer as she walked further away from the woman and man near the ring. She couldn't believe they hadn't noticed she was gone.

At last, she reached the entrance. It was a door, as she had hoped. But darkness loomed large inside of it. There was no light to be found. Did she dare go in anyway?

A shaky step forward answered that. Then another. And another. As she went, it became easier to see. It was like someone slowly was turning on the lights, but there were no lights.

How long was this tunnel, she wondered. She wished she had a snack. Long journeys were always better with snacks. She'd always gotten in trouble at the orphanage for hoarding food in her sock drawer. But in her defense, one never knew when one would need their next snack.

Her pulse skyrocketed as she heard yelling.

Uh-oh. They had probably noticed she was gone. She fought with her instincts. One half wanted her to freeze in place. The other wanted her to run. And she wasn't sure which was the right choice.

How angry might her new owners be about this little excursion? They wouldn't have a chance to take it out on her if they couldn't find her.

She ran.

Too late.

CHAPTER 24

JAMES

My pulse shot up. Silen.

In the kerfuffle, we'd forgotten all about him.

Trevor snapped his head around, vengeance burning in his beady reptilian eyes.

Brandon—who I still could not believe was really here, my friend from so long ago—looked to me, his eyes questioning.

Instinctively, I understood. His note had said to bring me. Kidnapping Luna and Silen had been a means to that end, though why he had gone about it that way I couldn't guess. Now I was here, so, for Brandon, Silen had served his purpose. He was wordlessly asking if Silen was still important to me.

I didn't even need to ponder to know the answer. Silen could *not* be on the loose. Even if none of the men and women here spilled our secrets, that man had no motivation not to. He was a menace.

"We have to find him," I said aloud.

Brandon nodded. He shot upright to full height and bellowed. "Tyler? Tyler!"

The guy that Adam had punched in the face stepped through the crowd, nursing a bruised and swollen left eye. That must have been Tyler. From the look of it, Adam had only winged him, but still managed to send him flying and mess him up like that. I shuddered a bit, contemplating how strong Adam really must be.

"Do you have scouts waiting for you outside that may have seen him?" Tyler said, addressing me while casting worried glances between Adam and Trevor. All three of us solemnly shook our heads. Inevitably, Adam and Trevor had just as much of a vendetta against Silen as I did. I would bet anything Luna regretted keeping him alive now.

Her eyes stayed locked on Adam. He stepped over and put his arm around her waist, squeezing her tight.

"Check the cameras!" Brandon ordered Tyler as he rushed through the crowd of teens toward the front door. "You, come with me," he ordered another of the boys about my age from the crowd.

Just when the adrenaline had been starting to wane.

Adam, Trevor, and I bolted out after him.

"We can resolve our differences later. Split up and search," Brandon instructed, directing us to each go in a different direction.

Trevor shifted the rest of the way to lizard immediately, not needing to be told twice, and zoomed off to the south on spindly lizard legs.

Adam glared at Brandon one final time, then appraised me quizzically. I nodded, and Adam accepted it wordlessly, if reluctantly, before darting to the west.

It was unfortunate that it hadn't rained or snowed. It would've been a lot easier to track him through footprints. I could shift and try to sniff him out, but I was absolutely not ready for that conversation with Brandon.

As Brandon and his assistant set off east and I took the north, I wondered how fast Silen could possibly move. He'd had the ATCV last time he was free. On foot, I couldn't imagine he'd have a successful getaway.

I considered what would happen if any of us ran into the mad scientist. I wasn't sure if Trevor would be strong enough to take down Silen himself, though, on second thought, his spite might be enough.

Maybe I should've been flattered that Brandon and Adam evidently thought I could take Silen alone. Realistically, I probably could, even if I didn't transform. I was itching to get my hands on him.

I trekked through a wooded area, wondering if I could just transform my nose for a better sense of smell. My control wasn't as good as that of Luna and the others who'd been Titans longer than me, sometimes by years, but I could maybe manage it. Maybe.

Scanning the ground with my eyes, I looked for any footprints that might fit Silen. He wasn't very heavy, and the ground was pretty hard from the cold. Even my shoes were leaving only a faint trace that I had stepped anywhere.

I hoped that the others were having better luck than I was. I would never forgive myself if he got away because of something that I missed.

A sudden noise and movement came from above me. I nearly jumped out of my skin. A few small twigs fell, and as I glanced around to see what had caused it, my gaze was met by a tiny, furry little creature.

The squirrel stared down at me, curiously tilting its head. My heartbeat was out of control.

This was stupid.

I decided that, at least for the time being, I would transform. Even if anyone else caught up with me, only Adam would know it was me. But I planned on them not catching up with me anyway. This way I could sniff out Silen, if he was indeed out this way, and return him to captivity where he belonged.

CHAPTER 25

LUNA

I saw Adam bolt out of the door behind James. I tried to follow them, but somebody stopped me, hand on my arm. I turned, ready to deck someone.

It was the guy who had kidnapped me, the one Brandon had called Tyler. He looked much worse for wear now that Adam had punched him. But I didn't want to be stuck here with him, even if he was maimed.

"Do you know where the guy who was with you went?" Tyler asked me.

I pushed to brush past him, but he held firm. I could've knocked him over, but I would feel bad about it. Didn't want to kick a man while he was down.

"Do you know where he went?" he demanded.

"No," I sneered. "But I could help find him if you'd get out of my way."

Tyler frowned, looking back toward the front door.

"I think you'd be more useful with me; there are people searching for him already. But like Brandon said, I can check the cameras and see where he went. And with your knowledge, maybe figure out where he'd be going."

"Why would I help you?" I spat out. "You kidnapped me."

"I'm sorry about that." He hung his head. "I was just doing my job. I understand if you don't want to rat out your friend, I just—"

I cut him off. "OH, he's *not* my friend."

The young man blinked rapidly, trying to process my vitriol.

"Oh, okay. So you will help?"

I sighed.

"It probably is best to not have him on the loose," I acquiesced.

I let him lead me to a surveillance room with a handful of screens, some headphones, and a transponder not unlike the one I had seen in James' possession a year ago.

He pulled out a chair for me, offering me a seat. A gentlemanly gesture for a kidnapper. I took it, though my suspiciousness lingered.

"I don't suppose you have cameras inside the attic?" I said derisively. I had no idea where Silen had run off to. Could he survive in the wild? I wasn't sure. Maybe all of this was overkill, considering James or Adam would most likely find him anyway. If they were going the right direction, that was.

Tyler handed me a pair of headphones and took one up for himself. I stared at him like he had two heads. He nudged them in my direction again. "This will help us communicate with the search party."

I rolled my eyes and accepted them, while simultaneously dreaming about how I could strangle him with his. I was so done with all of this.

Putting them on my ears made me feel antsy. I couldn't hear as much in the immediate world around me, so I uncovered my left ear. That way if this dude made any sudden moves, I'd be ready.

He didn't seem like the type to be in this line of work, and I wondered how he'd ended up getting a gig as an assistant kidnapper to begin with. Surely the government had better opportunities for guys like him?

I watched him work out of the corner of my eyes as I stared at the computer in front of me. There were two dots bobbing in different directions. One of the transponders crackled, and Tyler picked it up.

"Any leads based on footage?" Brandon's voice came through the headphones.

"Not yet, sir," Tyler said through the static. "I'm checking it now."

He clicked on one of the many small screens that showed live footage. As he ran the curser over the video, a small white bar formed at the bottom of the screen. I watched as he dragged the little dot that ran along the white bar to the left. It rewound the video, showing the group of guys leaving out of the front door. He rewound it further, combing through it meticulously. I looked at the computer in front of me. It had the same amount of small little rectangles of video.

I clicked a different one. It would actually be helpful to have Silen back. He was still a wealth of information, though not much good for ransom or anything. But first I'd punch his lights out for double-crossing me and leaving me like this.

I scrubbed through the video, searching for any movement. I wasn't sure where the location of this camera was, but it was outside of the building. It seemed like maybe it was facing the back? I went back to a few minutes prior, watching the assistant that Brandon had taken with him disappear into the thick of the woods in that direction. There was no sign of Silen, even after I backed it up further. I double-checked, not wanting to have missed something. It was hard to focus in these conditions. I didn't actually trust this guy, but a common enemy was a universal language.

I looked up, seeing a camera in the corner of the room. Man there were a lot of these things. Returning my attention to the monitor, I clicked out of the screen and went back to the cluttered chaos of a million little rectangles. I found the one that was pointed at us.

"I've checked this one." I pointed to my screen to show Tyler, that way we weren't dipping into the same feeds.

"How about you work from the bottom up, and I'll work from the top down," he suggested. He genuinely looked grateful for the help, and maybe a little green.

I was surprised, as we went through all these surveillance tapes, just how many cameras were in this place.

"How does the government afford all of these cameras for one little building?" I muttered out loud as I scanned through copious amounts of camera footage. This place was nowhere near the caliber of other facilities. I couldn't see how they had justified the expense.

"This mission was privately funded," Tyler said, almost as an afterthought as his fingers clicked the keys of his keyboard in rapid succession. His brow was furrowed, his face deeply troubled.

I stopped, sitting up a little straighter. What? Privately funded by who? Did that mean that all of this data, including our faces and information, were not going straight to the government? Not that they could really come and take us in Reunion City, but I'd sleep better at night knowing this was not going to be a safety setback, as I had originally anticipated.

Before I could start asking clarifying questions, Tyler turned to me, his face paling. "Did your companion actually make it out of the ceiling?"

I thought for a moment. I supposed I really didn't know, considering I had been detained pretty quickly. We were all just assuming that he had made it out, but had he? I had to suppress a giggle at the thought of Silen still crawling on his hands and knees across the ceiling beams.

"I think you'd know better than me," I said honestly. "It got pretty crazy when I fell through. I wasn't exactly keeping track of him."

"That may be true, but I was knocked out by your friend for like a minute, so I know even less."

My eyes got big. I couldn't exactly apologize—he did have it coming. So I just said, "Oh," then added, "Hazards of the job I guess," trying to lighten the quickly crashing mood.

"You have no idea, honestly." He brushed his hand down his face, wincing as it made contact with his bruise.

"I guess we could crawl up into the ceiling to look for him. Unless this privately funded mission has an infrared camera or something…"

Tyler looked thoughtful, but ultimately shook his head. "Don't think we remembered to pack anything like that. Doubt anyone thought we'd need it."

"That's unfortunate," I said. "Is there any way to get out of the ceiling besides the tiles going down into the building?"

"Not that I know of." Tyler cringed.

I sat back and thought. What would be a good way to flush Silen out without hurting anyone else in the building?

"Do you have a broom closet?"

"Oh, are you feeling domestic?" He laughed.

My eyes turned to slits as I glared at him.

"Very funny," I quipped. "I hope you remember that when I impale you with the back of a broom."

CHAPTER 26

SILEN

Silen could hear muffled conversations from beneath him. If he leaned forward and put his ear directly to the foam ceiling tile, bracing himself on beams, he could make out clearer words here and there. Some things he had to guess at, but from other conversations he'd gleaned enough that the information was clear. He could make out that his absence had caused a frenzied search party. It had made sense that they thought he'd escaped during the distraction of Luna falling through the ceiling.

But what they didn't know is that he was a little bit scared of heights. He'd intended to have Luna help him down when they escaped, but with her no longer in the picture, he'd have to figure it out himself. If he wasn't careful, he'd hurt himself. Bruises were such an inconvenience though. It wasn't fitting for someone with such perfect intellect to be brutalized like that.

Luna's voice perked his ears up. Perhaps she would be able to help him get down after all. He raised himself up, balancing more comfortably for a moment. The boy who had kidnapped them seemed to be with her, but she didn't sound in distress.

Silen took a deep breath, fighting the dust that made his eyes water, and leaned down once more. He even risked scooting a tile a centimeter over to hear a little better.

His eyes narrowed as he overheard their plan. They already suspected that he was still in the ceiling, which meant he had even less time than he had originally thought. They were planning on flushing him out by poking the ceiling tiles with a broom until they found him.

While he could've played cat and mouse with them, he didn't want to. He preferred to be on the other side of a game like that. He contemplated his options.

A chair scooting on the floor made him pay attention once more.

Were they leaving the room?

His ears strained, his breathing halted as he struggled to make out what was happening. His heartbeat was deafening in his ears. It irritated him as it interfered with his ability to tell what was going on. The door opened, and he could feel it in the beams that he leaned on. This could be his chance. The door closed. He was sure of it. But did they both leave? Or just one of them?

After a minute of painstakingly trying to hear, and being sure there was nothing, he took off the ceiling tile and peered into the room. Nobody. On a table sat two sets of computer monitors. Security camera monitors.

He carefully changed positions, swung his legs over the side, and made a snap decision. It was escape now or get captured. Bruises were better than captivity. Trying to land on the spinning chairs would only cause more damage.

He slid himself down as far as he could, so that when he touched down, it would make as little noise as possible. The solidity of the floor was an immediate relief to his muscles that had been under strain trying to balance on the beams. He extended his hands to brace himself as his system recalibrated.

Silen couldn't spend too much time stretching them out; he had to get going. He looked at the monitors, scoping out where Luna and the boy had gone in the building. He moved the footage back until he found the place where everyone had split up and made a mental note of the direction. He didn't know where he was going to go. He wouldn't go back to a government facility. He didn't want to be locked away again. Silen decided he would figure it out on the road. He saw on the camera that Luna and the boy were busy in the utility closet. Adrenaline pressed him forward. He was being sloppy and he knew it. But he had to get out of here. Sometimes having a plan was a problem that held you back.

He took one last look at the monitors. The coast was clear.

Opening the door like he belonged there, he walked calmly down the hall, out the front door, and straight ahead. The fresh air felt good in his lungs after the dust in the attic. He walked into the tree line across the gravel road. He checked his pocket for the vial, relieved to find it still there and intact despite all the crawling and acrobatics.

By the time they found him on the cameras, he would, with any luck, be long gone.

CHAPTER 27

CASSANDRA

Cassandra's lips were pursed. Her long, well-kept nails tapped on a manila folder sitting on the table as she stared down at the singed paper. This small, seemingly insignificant page presented a big, big problem.

When she'd allowed these mutants into her city, she hadn't anticipated the level of trouble they might cause. Or the potential threat they would pose. On a long enough timeline, they would overthrow her. And if they found out about her importing activity, they might not leave her alive. She had to get this situation under control. She just needed a little more information…

A young man poked his head into the room, an unasked question in his silence.

"Send him in," Cassandra instructed.

The boy did a slight bow and disappeared.

Moments later, Gregory Fitcher emerged from the doorway. "Greg," as Cassandra knew from his file he preferred to be called, looked out of place but at ease. He was an unpolished man, and a bit in awe of the fanciness of the office.

"Have a seat," Cassandra said through a polite, business-like smile.

The rectangular wooden table was long, with seats on every side. Greg chose to sit on the side opposite Cassandra, with his back to the large window to the outside. His face didn't display discomfort so much as confusion.

He fidgeted nervously as Cassandra eyed him.

"Can I get you something to drink?" she offered in a soothing tone.

"I'm alright, thank you," he declined politely, surveying the chandelier on the ceiling. Opulence may have been something he had never seen at all. Cassandra could see his family having been impoverished in the Before Time.

"Well." She plastered on another fake smile, ready to get the interrogation under way. "I just had a few questions for you, about the fire."

His eyes glazed over with a sadness that had been in the background before.

"Okay," he replied simply.

She leaned forward, reaching toward him in a comforting gesture, "I'm so sorry for the loss of the home your family loved. I hope they are resting comfortably in the hotel?"

He nodded silently in affirmation, before starting on his own line of questioning. "Is there any word on my brother-in-law?"

Alan Iverson. Cassandra already knew his name and didn't need it supplied. *According to his file*, he'd been missing since the house fire, but no remains had been found in the aftermath. According to his file, his whereabouts were unknown.

According to his file.

"Not yet," Cassandra answered, folding her hands. "But rest assured, we are still putting in every effort to find him."

Greg's face fell. It was clear that he cared very much for his family. And that could work in her favor. Perhaps he knew what all this was about.

"Have you ever seen this before?" She slid the paper across the table for him to see, keeping a finger on the top near where the Titan program symbol was printed. The burnt edges framed it, which seemed almost poetic. The program had, and always would be, surrounded by contention and the threat of violence and war.

She had no doubt that its legacy would continue.

Greg

Greg looked at the paper, his face questioning as he glanced between it and Cassandra. What was he supposed to see in this? It looked intimidating. Official. As he scrutinized it, he realized the symbol looked familiar. Like the scrap paper Meg had been drawing on.

"This is the paper my niece was drawing on before the fire," he stated, still confused.

"Is anything else significant about it?" Cassandra tilted her head as she asked.

"It's a little crispy," he stated simply, pointed to the edges.

A brief glimpse of annoyance crossed Cassandra's face, but she quickly concealed it. He guessed that hadn't been the right answer.

"You don't recognize this symbol?" Her nail dug into the paper, holding it in place.

"No," Greg said earnestly. "Should I? I mean, it kind of looks like an ankh, I guess... That's the word, right? I didn't actually pass my mythology class in college, but that seems like where I might've seen it."

Cassandra's expression softened.

"I'm just trying to get to the bottom of the house fire, and these papers in the wrong hands could've absolutely put a target on your family," she explained.

Greg bristled. "My family wouldn't have been involved in anything bad. Somebody must have planted them there."

Cassandra

That was a good thought. And one Cassandra had considered. Was it possible Titania had placed the papers there while she was rescuing the child? It would've certainly been a good chance to burn papers she shouldn't have had in the first place. But considering she could burn anything on contact, it didn't seem necessary. Something wasn't adding up.

"That was awfully kind of your neighbor to rescue your niece," Cassandra said, changing the subject. "You must be really close."

His face brightened. "She's a great neighbor; she and her friends are so young and energetic. I'm indebted to her for saving my niece. That was selfless of her, but it doesn't surprise me at all. She's a wonderful young lady."

Cassandra nodded along like she was listening to a grandpa talk about his granddaughter. She wore a strained smile, showing interest enough to keep him talking in hopes some helpful information would come out next.

"I'm still just so shocked that she didn't sustain a single injury while rescuing your niece. That's so peculiar, isn't it?" she probed.

"I think she's got a guardian angel," Greg said with a smile. "How else do you explain it?"

Cassandra gave him a placating smile. He was annoyingly naive. Either that or this was an act. Either way, she'd be keeping a much closer eye on him. And she knew just how to do it.

"Well, Greg, I so appreciate you coming today. I don't want to take too much of your time. There's just one other thing."

She reached for the folder that had sat closed on the table the entire meeting and flipped it open. Inside was a simple form printed on cream paper, and one gold card about the size of her palm.

"Greg," Cassandra said, sliding the card across the table. "I was thinking what a wonderful addition you would be to the Haven Club."

"Oh, I could never afford..." began Greg in response.

"I'm willing to sponsor your application," said Cassandra, cutting him off. "And the annual fees, if necessary." She smiled a smile of practiced sweetness. "That's how much I—*we*—would welcome your membership."

She tugged the paper for the membership application out of the folder. Her hands faltered as she took in Greg's frown.

"What's the matter?" she inquired with some genuine surprise.

"Oh." Greg shifted. "It's just that…you know how clubs are."

"…How clubs *are*?" Cassandra blinked, her mouth slightly agape.

He nodded. "Sometimes exclusive membership to something isn't all it's cracked up to be. By the time you're in, you're more valuable to them than they are to you…"

Greg was rambling.

"You think you're valuable?" Cassandra forced a sense of demureness into her voice. A plain, poised look on her face. She couldn't understand what he was talking about, and her curiosity was greater than her disgust.

"No, no," he said, waving his hands in a dismissive manner. "I was just musing about how clubs usually work."

"Ah, well then…" she began sliding the paper toward him. But he pushed his chair out instead, moving to stand.

"I'm afraid I can't accept. I'm not even sure if I morally agree with clubs, you know? Excluding other people. No, I mean, I'm not saying anything against Haven, of course…"

"Of course." Cassandra's eyes narrowed as she snatched the paper back and pressed it into the folder once more.

"And like I said," Greg mused as he walked toward the door, "I'm not valuable enough for them, anyway."

"I understand," Cassandra said simply.

A bemused smile crawled across his face. "I'm glad you do. I knew you would."

This was a dead end. But that was no matter…

She needed to pay another visit to Greg's brother-in-law, Alan.

CHAPTER 30

JAMES

Brandon stared defiantly at Adam. I gulped. I was going to end up bloody and bruised by the time this discussion was over, I just knew it. I just didn't know if it was going to be by Brandon, Adam, or both.

Adam had called off the search for Silen after we'd spent most of the afternoon on it with no results. Now, without that distraction, it was time to address the elephant in the room. Well, *herd* of elephants.

Brandon had led us to a conference room and beckoned us to sit at a large wooden table. Adam was loathe to take a single step further without answers, but he begrudgingly allowed it. His mood did not improve during the short walk.

"Do you want to tell me why you kidnapped my girlfriend?" Adam asked, way too calmly compared to his actions when we had arrived. "I'd love to hear an explanation."

Brandon looked pensive, his lips unmoving.

"Answer me!" Adam slammed his fist into the table. My eyes went wide. This was a side of him I hadn't seen until today. I didn't know he had it in him.

Brandon sighed, looking toward me. "You know, I have some questions. too."

My heart raced. Was this the same man I had known? Could we safely answer his questions? I had called him for help a year ago, but I'd thought I hadn't gotten through. Maybe I had, and maybe he wasn't who I had known him to be.

Maybe Titania had been right.

"What's with all the human-animal hybrids?" Brandon pressed, glancing across the room at Trevor, who was the only one not to have taken a seat. He stood leaning up against the wall with his arms crossed. He had fully reverted to human, but at the mention of hybrids he lolled a forked lizard tongue out and leered at Brandon.

"Did you do that? Create them, I mean?" Brandon asked, turning to look at me with disbelief in his eyes.

Adam's voice overlapped mine as we both spoke.

"No, of course not," I said.

"I asked the first question!" Adam interjected.

Brandon glowered at Adam, then looked at me again. "Then who did?"

"I…was hoping you'd have more information than we do," I said sheepishly.

Brandon threw his right hand up in the air and then laid it on the table. It sounded heavy. Was he in armor or something?

"So you didn't know about any of this?" I asked him, not wanting to let on that I was also spliced now. When we'd last spoken, years ago and before I had even met Titania, I hadn't been.

"No, dude, I had no idea there were human-animal hybrids. Whose idea was that? The government's? Seems to me they have a lot of ideas that we're all supposed to participate in but know little to nothing about, and I am not too sure how I feel about that at the moment."

"Great," Trevor huffed. "Nobody knows anything. Imagine that."

My head began to throb. I rubbed at my temple, staring blankly down at the table. Seeing Brandon, I had hoped he would be able to shed some light on the situation, not muddy the waters. At least we knew he wasn't too thrilled with the government either.

"So what are we going to do?" I asked, the question directed at both Brandon and Adam. They were the hotheads. They were the strong personalities. They would have to agree on what happened next, otherwise it would just be a tug-of-war. If we were even going to be in this together to begin with. I still felt like Adam might just pounce on Brandon at any second. He was shaking, with rage or adrenaline—I couldn't tell which.

"I suppose that depends on what we're wanting to accomplish," sighed Brandon.

"Hey!" Adam barked. At long last Brandon turned to acknowledge him. "The only reason you still have lips is because *he* knows you," Adam said, jerking his thumb at me, "but if you don't use them to tell me what YOU were trying to accomplish by kidnapping my girlfriend and the lunatic that you let get away, I will personally see how far they can stretch before your friends all think I spliced you with aardvark DNA!"

Brandon's gaze remained unchanged, which I knew would only goad Adam more. This conversation needed to be moved along, fast.

"Are you still working for them? The government, I mean?" I asked and then grimaced. That seemed like the next logical, most important piece of information to glean. He clearly was unsure of how he felt about the government, but that didn't mean he was free from their influence.

"Yes," Brandon admitted simply.

Adam shot me a glance that said, *See, we can't trust him*! but I ignored it as I tried to think all of this through.

"What do they have you doing? Do they know you're here? Did they know about you capturing Luna? Do they know she is here?"

I couldn't think of a way for them to not be aware of this, given all the other people that were in this building.

"They know as little as possible to allow me to get away for a while. They think I'm conducting some research that will benefit them. I got a grant for it and everything," Brandon answered. "I was even able to hire away some of their employees for my own crew with the money. Just some that I trust."

"So you know and control everyone here?" Adam clarified.

"As much as anyone can know or control another human being, I suppose," Brandon said.

"How many of them know about Luna and Titania being hybrids, or the Titan project as a whole?" I asked.

Trevor's eyes shifted nervously between the two of us. I knew how conflicted he felt about being a Titan, and how protective he was of them all despite those feelings.

"The fire girl?" asked Brandon. "Well, one of them knows most everything, the rest know as little as possible."

"Which one knows everything?" I asked.

"The one that your friend knocked into next week," Brandon said flatly.

I grimaced.

Adam just sat back and laughed. "Maybe he won't remember anything once he's slept off his concussion. Then all that's left is to swear you to silence." Adam fixed Brandon with a threatening gaze.

"Let's just be calm," I pleaded with him. "We can figure this out."

"When you called me a year ago," Brandon said, looking directly at me, "you asked for help. I didn't know if you needed help getting away from the fire and wolf girls or help *for* them. I was doing the best I could given the information I had." He paused and shot a look back at Adam. "I never intended to kidnap anyone's girlfriend."

ADAM

Six of us across two ATCVs shot through the night on the way back to Reunion City. Brandon had been all too eager for us to leave, once he'd ascertained that James was not and never had been our captive. The only problem was that he had insisted on coming along as well, which he argued was to help us out to pay us back for our trouble.

I knew better, of course. He wanted to ensure that James was not under duress and was actually doing fine.

I allowed it for my own secret reason: I needed to be able to keep an eye on him. Our time together may have been brief so far, but I already knew that he could be a formidable opponent if he wanted to be. This way he would be close enough to monitor.

I made James ride on the fancier ATCV with him while Luna and Trevor joined me. Nothing personal, it's just that Brandon was his friend, while the rest of us weren't quite ready to move him out of the enemy category yet.

The kid whose block I'd knocked off was the sixth of us, and he rode along with James and Brandon. I ignored him, mostly.

I'd already made a compelling argument that he should leave us alone, and despite my quip earlier, I doubted he'd be forgetting anytime soon.

My thoughts turned back to the road ahead.

Stepping back into town was going to be a relief with Luna in tow. My legs ached to be there, walking back into the apartments. I could not believe Luna had gotten kidnapped. She wasn't a damsel in distress, she was a warrior. She must've really gotten snuck up on for this to have happened. But I had to admit, it was nice to be able to be her knight in shining armor, swooping in to rescue her, just this once. These opportunities were thankfully few and far between, but I believed it was a part of every man to want to save his lady.

I couldn't have cared less that Silen got away, for the most part. I had no confidence that he would make it anywhere alive on his own. Whatever usefulness he had provided had been greatly exaggerated in my estimation. And the area we'd been in was fairly remote. There was no way he'd ask for help getting to safety. His ego wouldn't let him, and that was provided that he could even find his way back to a road.

He was a dead man walking.

The buildings of the city jutted out as they came into view, carving the skyline into jagged pieces as we went. It was weird to call this place home. To live around so many other people, outside of a compound. Out in the open. Granted, we weren't always in transformation, but still. Despite being a patchwork of people and ideas, I didn't mind it. I just wished that I could offer Luna something better. I supposed a city was an upgrade compared to a cave, though.

"Almost there," Trevor murmured.

We were all exhausted, and I was no exception. I had maybe gone a little too hard in my show of force. There was a distinct possibility that I would have some bruising, or at the very least, more extreme soreness in the morning. But, for now, I pulled Luna in close, holding her to my chest. She sighed, leaning into me. If the other boys were surprised by this, they didn't say anything. This was a mind-your-own-business moment.

We started the descent down into the city when I heard it.

Except I wasn't sure what *it* was.

Something akin to a greeting, maybe? I stiffened up, looking around. But nobody else seemed to be hearing it. Was I going crazy?

"Are you okay?" Luna asked sleepily.

"I'm fine," I assured her, tucking her back into my chest.

I sent out a mental message to see if it would happen again. Thirty seconds ticked by and I was quickly convincing myself I hadn't heard anything at all.

Then it happened again.

<Who are you?> I sent out.

I couldn't speak to just anyone or anything. I couldn't *hear* just anyone or anything. This had to be another Titan. That was probably it. Maybe this one was a baby, because whatever it was saying, I didn't understand it. I made a mental note to ask Jen. They must've taken in someone new while we were gone. I couldn't imagine where from, but life was full of surprises right now.

There was a bit of babbling at the edge of my awareness, but every time I tried to respond, it stopped. I supposed I would meet the newcomer soon enough.

CHAPTER 28

JAMES

The search party returned empty-handed. I couldn't tell who was more upset by it. We'd been gone long enough that we'd have to drive home in the dark. It had been a valiant effort.

I'd tried to stay in transformation for as long as I could on the trek back, hoping to pick up that devil's scent. But there was nothing. At least not close enough that I could smell. It was a funny sight to walk in and see Luna and Tyler, face still swollen and everything, poking the ceiling tiles with broomsticks. I could just see them nailing Silen with a kidney shot. The thought pleased me.

"Covering all your bases?" I asked, crossing my arms.

I could tell Luna wanted to growl at me, but she kept her composure.

"We checked the cameras," Tyler said, eying me warily, "and didn't see where that guy escaped to, so we thought it would be best to just make sure he wasn't actually hiding in the ceiling."

"That would explain why none of us found him." I frowned, looking up suspiciously.

Perhaps someone ought to go up there and check it out…but it wasn't going to be me. Too bad we didn't have Natalie with us; she'd be the perfect person for this job.

"So, who's getting up there?" I prodded.

"Not me," Luna stated firmly. Tyler still just blinked at me with his one working lid.

Adam and the rest of the search party entered the building, and as they took in Luna playing Whac-A-Mole with the ceiling tiles, they wore matching quizzical expressions.

"They think he's in the ceiling," I said, catching them up to speed.

"Oh," Brandon said, unfazed. "Let's send a drone up in there. It'll only take a minute or two to scan the whole thing."

I was flabbergasted that he thought of that. It was a much more efficient idea than poking ceiling tiles. Not that Luna wasn't providing creative solutions…

CHAPTER 29

SILEN

Silen stumbled across the countryside with no firm plan in place, only relief that he'd managed to perfectly evade the search party. Between the data he had gleaned about camera placement from the computer display, and positioning himself in the middle of two directions of the search, he'd successfully avoided detection.

So now what? He thought that perhaps he could find somewhere like Reunion City, where no one would have to know who, or what, he was. He wouldn't go back under the watch of the government, and he could start all over.

What would he do, now that he had been given the serendipitous opportunity to exercise self-determination again? The idea stopped him in his tracks, derailing his insistent steps. It was hard to think about. Life had never gone the way he had wanted it to. Not by a long shot.

He would just keep walking. One foot in front of the other. He'd made it out of bad situations before. He could do it again. And this time, he didn't have anything to lose.

CHAPTER 30

JAMES

Brandon stared defiantly at Adam. I gulped. I was going to end up bloody and bruised by the time this discussion was over, I just knew it. I just didn't know if it was going to be by Brandon, Adam, or both.

Adam had called off the search for Silen after we'd spent most of the afternoon on it with no results. Now, without that distraction, it was time to address the elephant in the room. Well, *herd* of elephants.

Brandon had led us to a conference room and beckoned us to sit at a large wooden table. Adam was loathe to take a single step further without answers, but he begrudgingly allowed it. His mood did not improve during the short walk.

"Do you want to tell me why you kidnapped my girlfriend?" Adam asked, way too calmly compared to his actions when we had arrived. "I'd love to hear an explanation."

Brandon looked pensive, his lips unmoving.

"Answer me!" Adam slammed his fist into the table. My eyes went wide. This was a side of him I hadn't seen until today. I didn't know he had it in him.

Brandon sighed, looking toward me. "You know, I have some questions. too."

My heart raced. Was this the same man I had known? Could we safely answer his questions? I had called him for help a year ago, but I'd thought I hadn't gotten through. Maybe I had, and maybe he wasn't who I had known him to be.

Maybe Titania had been right.

"What's with all the human-animal hybrids?" Brandon pressed, glancing across the room at Trevor, who was the only one not to have taken a seat. He stood leaning up against the wall with his arms crossed. He had fully reverted to human, but at the mention of hybrids he lolled a forked lizard tongue out and leered at Brandon.

"Did you do that? Create them, I mean?" Brandon asked, turning to look at me with disbelief in his eyes.

Adam's voice overlapped mine as we both spoke.

"No, of course not," I said.

"I asked the first question!" Adam interjected.

Brandon glowered at Adam, then looked at me again. "Then who did?"

"I…was hoping you'd have more information than we do," I said sheepishly.

Brandon threw his right hand up in the air and then laid it on the table. It sounded heavy. Was he in armor or something?

"So you didn't know about any of this?" I asked him, not wanting to let on that I was also spliced now. When we'd last spoken, years ago and before I had even met Titania, I hadn't been.

"No, dude, I had no idea there were human-animal hybrids. Whose idea was that? The government's? Seems to me they have a lot of ideas that we're all supposed to participate in but know little to nothing about, and I am not too sure how I feel about that at the moment."

"Great," Trevor huffed. "Nobody knows anything. Imagine that."

My head began to throb. I rubbed at my temple, staring blankly down at the table. Seeing Brandon, I had hoped he would be able to shed some light on the situation, not muddy the waters. At least we knew he wasn't too thrilled with the government either.

"So what are we going to do?" I asked, the question directed at both Brandon and Adam. They were the hotheads. They were the strong personalities. They would have to agree on what happened next, otherwise it would just be a tug-of-war. If we were even going to be in this together to begin with. I still felt like Adam might just pounce on Brandon at any second. He was shaking, with rage or adrenaline—I couldn't tell which.

"I suppose that depends on what we're wanting to accomplish," sighed Brandon.

"Hey!" Adam barked. At long last Brandon turned to acknowledge him. "The only reason you still have lips is because *he* knows you," Adam said, jerking his thumb at me, "but if you don't use them to tell me what YOU were trying to accomplish by kidnapping my girlfriend and the lunatic that you let get away, I will personally see how far they can stretch before your friends all think I spliced you with aardvark DNA!"

Brandon's gaze remained unchanged, which I knew would only goad Adam more. This conversation needed to be moved along, fast.

"Are you still working for them? The government, I mean?" I asked and then grimaced. That seemed like the next logical, most important piece of information to glean. He clearly was unsure of how he felt about the government, but that didn't mean he was free from their influence.

"Yes," Brandon admitted simply.

Adam shot me a glance that said, *See, we can't trust him*! but I ignored it as I tried to think all of this through.

"What do they have you doing? Do they know you're here? Did they know about you capturing Luna? Do they know she is here?"

I couldn't think of a way for them to not be aware of this, given all the other people that were in this building.

"They know as little as possible to allow me to get away for a while. They think I'm conducting some research that will benefit them. I got a grant for it and everything," Brandon answered. "I was even able to hire away some of their employees for my own crew with the money. Just some that I trust."

"So you know and control everyone here?" Adam clarified.

"As much as anyone can know or control another human being, I suppose," Brandon said.

"How many of them know about Luna and Titania being hybrids, or the Titan project as a whole?" I asked.

Trevor's eyes shifted nervously between the two of us. I knew how conflicted he felt about being a Titan, and how protective he was of them all despite those feelings.

"The fire girl?" asked Brandon. "Well, one of them knows most everything, the rest know as little as possible."

"Which one knows everything?" I asked.

"The one that your friend knocked into next week," Brandon said flatly.

I grimaced.

Adam just sat back and laughed. "Maybe he won't remember anything once he's slept off his concussion. Then all that's left is to swear you to silence." Adam fixed Brandon with a threatening gaze.

"Let's just be calm," I pleaded with him. "We can figure this out."

"When you called me a year ago," Brandon said, looking directly at me, "you asked for help. I didn't know if you needed help getting away from the fire and wolf girls or help *for* them. I was doing the best I could given the information I had." He paused and shot a look back at Adam. "I never intended to kidnap anyone's girlfriend."

ADAM

Six of us across two ATCVs shot through the night on the way back to Reunion City. Brandon had been all too eager for us to leave, once he'd ascertained that James was not and never had been our captive. The only problem was that he had insisted on coming along as well, which he argued was to help us out to pay us back for our trouble.

I knew better, of course. He wanted to ensure that James was not under duress and was actually doing fine.

I allowed it for my own secret reason: I needed to be able to keep an eye on him. Our time together may have been brief so far, but I already knew that he could be a formidable opponent if he wanted to be. This way he would be close enough to monitor.

I made James ride on the fancier ATCV with him while Luna and Trevor joined me. Nothing personal, it's just that Brandon was his friend, while the rest of us weren't quite ready to move him out of the enemy category yet.

The kid whose block I'd knocked off was the sixth of us, and he rode along with James and Brandon. I ignored him, mostly.

I'd already made a compelling argument that he should leave us alone, and despite my quip earlier, I doubted he'd be forgetting anytime soon.

My thoughts turned back to the road ahead.

Stepping back into town was going to be a relief with Luna in tow. My legs ached to be there, walking back into the apartments. I could not believe Luna had gotten kidnapped. She wasn't a damsel in distress, she was a warrior. She must've really gotten snuck up on for this to have happened. But I had to admit, it was nice to be able to be her knight in shining armor, swooping in to rescue her, just this once. These opportunities were thankfully few and far between, but I believed it was a part of every man to want to save his lady.

I couldn't have cared less that Silen got away, for the most part. I had no confidence that he would make it anywhere alive on his own. Whatever usefulness he had provided had been greatly exaggerated in my estimation. And the area we'd been in was fairly remote. There was no way he'd ask for help getting to safety. His ego wouldn't let him, and that was provided that he could even find his way back to a road.

He was a dead man walking.

The buildings of the city jutted out as they came into view, carving the skyline into jagged pieces as we went. It was weird to call this place home. To live around so many other people, outside of a compound. Out in the open. Granted, we weren't always in transformation, but still. Despite being a patchwork of people and ideas, I didn't mind it. I just wished that I could offer Luna something better. I supposed a city was an upgrade compared to a cave, though.

"Almost there," Trevor murmured.

We were all exhausted, and I was no exception. I had maybe gone a little too hard in my show of force. There was a distinct possibility that I would have some bruising, or at the very least, more extreme soreness in the morning. But, for now, I pulled Luna in close, holding her to my chest. She sighed, leaning into me. If the other boys were surprised by this, they didn't say anything. This was a mind-your-own-business moment.

We started the descent down into the city when I heard it.

Except I wasn't sure what *it* was.

Something akin to a greeting, maybe? I stiffened up, looking around. But nobody else seemed to be hearing it. Was I going crazy?

"Are you okay?" Luna asked sleepily.

"I'm fine," I assured her, tucking her back into my chest.

I sent out a mental message to see if it would happen again. Thirty seconds ticked by and I was quickly convincing myself I hadn't heard anything at all.

Then it happened again.

<Who are you?> I sent out.

I couldn't speak to just anyone or anything. I couldn't *hear* just anyone or anything. This had to be another Titan. That was probably it. Maybe this one was a baby, because whatever it was saying, I didn't understand it. I made a mental note to ask Jen. They must've taken in someone new while we were gone. I couldn't imagine where from, but life was full of surprises right now.

There was a bit of babbling at the edge of my awareness, but every time I tried to respond, it stopped. I supposed I would meet the newcomer soon enough.

CHAPTER 32

JAMES

"You're back!" Titania said, wrapping her arms around my neck. I fought the urge to pick her up and hold her. She probably wouldn't like to be scooped up like that, but my instincts were so much stronger now with two extra sets of DNA running around.

I squeezed her, in a way that I hoped wasn't too tight. "Did you miss me?"

She suddenly became aloof. But it was playful, not serious as it always had been before, when she was keeping her Titan nature secret from me.

"I guess so." She gave a teasing shrug.

"Did I miss anything exciting?" I asked teasingly.

She blanched a little. Uh-oh. We'd already had enough excitement to last a while.

"What?" I asked anxiously. "What happened?"

That caught the attention of the entire caravan.

"Is Miranda okay?" Trevor demanded.

"Oh, yes," Titania assured him. "Everyone is fine. There was just a house fire, Cassandra is acting a little funny, and we've had some people getting a little too close to home base recently. Just some teenagers doing some urban exploring, according to Jen and Natalie," she explained.

Adam looked between her and me.

"How close did they get?" he asked, suddenly on edge.

"Just a few blocks," Titania assured him. "And they're just kids. But that's not why Cassandra's upset. I rescued a little girl from a house fire, which I actually need to talk to you about…"

"Let's do it," I broke in as I noticed Brandon staring a hole right through her. "I just need to get some things handled first."

I grabbed Brandon and dragged him along with me. He was getting shut in my apartment until we talked all of this out, and I wasn't wasting any time getting him away from everyone else for now.

"I'll be with you ASAP," I told Titania, seeing her downcast expression, along with the quizzical glances she shot at Brandon. "Trust me, there's an order of operations I'm trying to observe here."

Brandon's bruised friend hurried after us. The ride back had been quiet, but I had at least learned that his name was Tyler.

He whispered something to Brandon, not loud enough for me to hear.

Brandon nodded discreetly. "I'll call you if I need you."

My curiosity was piqued, but I let it go. With that, Tyler was off into the night, into the greater city. And Brandon and I were off to my apartment.

CHAPTER 33

LUNA

The second everyone else left for their own places, Adam whisked me away and out of sight. I often forgot how strong he was until he hauled me off my feet in an instant and started casually walking down the street like I was weightless. I was a little jealous. I needed to start curling the kids or something.

"I'm sorry," I said, leaning into him as we went. I was so ashamed that I'd gotten caught. I couldn't believe it. And I couldn't believe they'd decided to bring Silen along as well. The only thing worse than getting kidnapped was getting kidnapped with Silen. He was insufferable. I couldn't believe he'd gotten away, either. I was sure that would come back to bite us in the butt somehow. But we should be safe here.

I didn't know if Adam was upset *with* me or upset *for* me, but the wrinkles on his face were deep.

"You don't need to be sorry."

I was caught off guard by that. He wasn't a drill sergeant by any means; in fact, if he wasn't close to you, it was hard to know him very well. He was quiet. Stoic. A little scary at times.

There were questions I wanted to ask that I just couldn't. There was so much about his past that was painful for him. It felt like poking at scars and asking if they hurt to try and pry into things. But typically, he would've been livid about something like this. Would've had me do more training. He'd always taught me to watch my back, to never let my guard down.

But now that I looked back on it, I *had* let my guard down. This corner of the city felt like a place where I could do that. Nobody knew we were here, except for Cassandra, and nobody had any reason to cause us trouble.

Except, apparently, for James'…whatever he was. That would be something that we would all have to contend with later. For now, James had vouched for him. Even so, Adam told James to keep the guy away from our hideout. None of us trusted him. Adam had gotten some good licks in though, and I doubted very highly that the man would want a round two with him.

"I'll be more careful," I promised as we reached the edge of the forest. There was a little clearing just inside that we'd found on a walk. Adam put me down on a log and shucked his shoes, dipping his feet into the freezing water. I shivered just watching him. His temperature regulation was otherworldly. I didn't understand it at all.

He sat, silently staring into the surface of the stream. The greens of the moss didn't look quite right, but then again, nothing really looked right anymore. At least it wasn't those glowy purple mushrooms that we'd encountered before.

I couldn't imagine eating one of those and becoming radioactive, if one would even survive such an encounter.

"You shouldn't have to be," Adam said, his voice a low rumble. He brushed his hair back. It was getting longer by the day.

I wished he would let me braid it, but he always said no, or "maybe someday." But he'd never tell me when.

I didn't know what to say. I couldn't see how things could continue like this. It felt like us against the world, even with the other Titans. Some days they seemed more of a liability than not, but the one thing that Adam had really wanted was companionship. That's what he'd told me after he rescued me the first time. He had been so unsure who to trust.

That was something I related to all too well. All it took was trusting the wrong person one time to change your life.

I had made that mistake. So many of us Titans had. And for us, the damage was irreversible.

"Any new breakthroughs in your research while I was gone?" I teased as I lowered myself to sit beside him. He nuzzled into my hair.

I doubted he'd had much time to research. I still needed to be filled in on how their mission in search of an antidote went. I had glimpsed Melody in the gym before we took off, but she was still in a wheelchair, which meant she still had a fish tail. I reasoned that no one had died, but it didn't look like they'd found an antidote either. Nothing gained, nothing lost sounded like a fair trade to me.

Adam scoffed, pulling away for a moment to fix me with a glare before his eyes softened again and he returned to hugging me.

I wondered what Adam's ultimate goal was with rescuing others. Would we all go our separate ways someday? Would we make our own city? It hurt my head to think about. A future that was hazy with impossibility.

"Whatever happens, I need you to take care of yourself," Adam said, pulling away for the second time and staring into my eyes with an intensity that I had only ever received from him. "I cannot lose you like that again."

His hands were gripping my shoulders firmly. I tried to ignore how hard he was holding me. Sometimes Adam could be like a puppy—he didn't know his own strength.

"You know I will," I assured him. Shame graced my cheeks with a burning glow. I hadn't this time, but this was the first and only time.

He held me so tightly I struggled to breathe.

"Are you alright?" I asked. He could be affectionate when it was just the two of us, but this was intense.

"I just need *you* to be alright," he whispered in my ear.

CHAPTER 34

TYLER

Stepping into the oversized and overdecorated hub of the city felt suffocating. I'd seen so much in the last year, in the last *day*, and this one wasn't even over yet, despite how badly my whole body hurt from the beating I'd taken just hours before. It was hard to be impressed by the opulent chandeliers and fancy rugs when things haunted my mind that I wished I could forget. I wished I could believe that Cassandra was just blind to the realities outside of this tower of hers, but I knew that wasn't true. The more time went on, the less I could justify the work I was doing for her.

I jabbed the elevator button with the full force of my frustration as I waited for the large metal doors to open. The night crew milled about in the lobby, reminding me that the city—and this tower in particular—never slept. I wasn't actually sure whether Cassandra herself ever slept, either.

The mission to find Brandon's buddy had been just another nudge toward uncertainty about what I was doing for him, and for Cassandra. I told myself there were no right or wrong jobs, just jobs. Everyone had to feed themselves, right?

I was beginning to believe that less and less, though. I had some hope that Brandon's intentions were good, but with Cassandra? I knew that was delusional to think. She was self-centered and self-serving, from what I could tell.

The elevator doors closed, temporarily trapping me inside as the cage ascended to the top floor.

They opened to Cassandra standing on the other side, arms crossed and lips forming a straight line across her mouth.

I inhaled deeply through my nose, the dusty smell of the powder they used to clean the carpets filling my nostrils. It was putrid, much like I was certain this conversation was about to be.

"You're back," she said, stepping to the side as she ushered me into her office. The same office where she had shouted me down not that long ago.

White papers caught my eye as they were strung out across the normally very clean desk. She must've been in the middle of something.

"I am, did you miss me?" I smiled, and though it was easily passing for genuine, I did not mean it.

My hand grasped the back of one of the chairs. I pulled it out and sat down, reclining comfortably before looking at her.

"Where were you?" she asked, her eyes immediately catching the fresh bruising on my face.

What a warm welcome.

"Not on the clock with you."

A year ago, I wouldn't have told her that. A year ago, I would've been worried about my job. But now? I didn't care.

Fire me. Maybe the half-humans would take me in; I trusted them more than I trusted government jobs at this point.

"I don't know why you feel the need to have an additional job." She stepped closer, fixing me with her unusual purple eyes. "Am I not paying you enough?"

I kept my mouth shut. She wanted me to talk, and I wasn't going to play ball on that.

She frowned, eyes narrowing to slits as she walked to her desk and gathered her papers.

"What if I offered you a spot in the Haven Club? Free, of course, and I just happen to have an application handy..." Her purple pupils darted unnaturally quickly over to a folder that lay alone on the table I was sitting next to, then back to me. It always made my skin crawl when her eyes did that.

"The perks go far beyond your pay right now. I really need employees I can count on. I want you to feel like all of your needs are met."

"I'll think about it," I said, again contemplating what my answer would've been a year ago. I didn't think there was anything she could offer me now that would make me want to stay with her.

"Why don't you sleep on it." She bit her lip. I wasn't used to seeing her act like this. Anxious, it seemed. "I'm sure you're tired from your other job and traveling."

There it was.

"I am tired," I said, taking my out. "I'll see you later."

CHAPTER 35

ADAM

After the rush of the happy reunion had died down and everyone else had gone to bed, but before I could start working through the logistics of what our next steps were with this new guy and his metal arm, I decided to go investigate something that pressed on my anxiety much worse than that. There would be time to decompress later. I needed an answer about who, or what, I was hearing since we'd returned.

I made sure that Luna was safely tucked away in the apartment. I told everyone I was going for a walk to clear my head. And, make no mistake, my head did need clearing. but my real purpose was to track down the voice that I continued to hear. Though I couldn't make out the language, it seemed to be a very young child. My thoughts raced as though they were cars speeding down a track, narrowly avoiding collision as they carelessly barreled forward. Who was this? Where were they? How had they gotten here? Jen hadn't said a word to me about anyone new. And she knew how I felt about new people. When I'd popped my head into the gym, everything was exactly as I had left it. Calmer, actually, considering all the little ones were asleep.

I trudged into the bleak streets, hoping that the child would go into a babbling spell. Exhaustion clawed at the base of my eyes. I shouldn't have gone so hard. But with the blinding hot rage that seared my mind when I saw Luna's captor, I couldn't stop myself. I was so used to stuffing down my anger. Restraining myself. Denying the conglomerate of instincts I held inside. I knew that I needed to release it slowly so that it couldn't build to this point, but I couldn't be reasoned with when Luna's welfare was on the line like that.

She was so tired, she'd barely wanted to talk on the way home. She kept saying she'd tell me everything later. I took it for genuine; I didn't get the sense that she was trying to keep anything from the others.

The streets were all the same lackluster gray. I wandered, taking in the symmetrical, cookie-cutter nature of the buildings scraping the sky. I walked toward the residential neighborhood. I hadn't explored that area much. I was surprised to find scattered ashes as the wind blew. I looked up to find a burned-down house. Is this what Titania had mentioned?

But there was no time to reflect on that, because suddenly the voice picked up. It was more babbling. I listened intently, trying to figure out what direction was the strongest. The repetitive sounds made it seem like it might be a song being sung over and over.

I followed it until it was so strong I felt like I was in the same room as the voice. But there was nothing. I was in the middle of a street with abandoned buildings on either side. I checked the insides, testing the door handles and briefly stepping through the remains of papers or wood or drywall that littered the floor. Both buildings came up completely empty.

But the voice remained. I looked down to find I was standing on top of a sewer drain. Could it be?

I gulped. I wasn't sure I could fit through there. I wasn't necessarily a claustrophobic person, but I wasn't keen on being in a tight space that I might not be able to get back out of. And if anyone had been watching me, it would look conspicuous for me to change form and return. I stayed the course, wedging my fingers underneath the rim and removing it. The voice got louder. Whatever it was, it was definitely down there.

I closed my eyes, took a deep breath, and tried to make myself as small as possible. The ladder that descended under the manhole was of questionable quality, but thankfully, it did not break under my weight. I should've brought someone like Natalie with me. But I didn't want to drag anyone else into my paranoia. It wouldn't be the first time, if it turned out to be nothing, that the foreign DNA had tricked my mind. It was better to just investigate on my own.

It wasn't well-lit, but my eyes had an easy time adjusting to the darkness. There was a small strip of concrete along the wall that I could walk down. It smelled absolutely rank. I should've tied my hair back before attempting something like this, but I hadn't known I'd be wallowing in filth.

After I shrugged off the sludge that had stuck to me on the descent, I took off down the concrete floor in pursuit of the voice. Just as I felt like I was getting somewhere, the thing, whatever it was, stopped babbling. I found myself in the dark, and unsure of which way to go. I decided to keep looking in the direction that

I was headed, because I was pretty sure it was the direction that I could hear things from.

I walked for what must have been a mile before I finally stumbled upon an ornate door. It was seemingly steel, with gold accents stretching from the corners to the center. The handle was connected to a black device of some kind. I examined it more closely and found a slot about three or four inches wide and a millimeter thick.

What on earth? Was this a card reader? Why would a card reader be installed on a door underneath the city?

The handle wouldn't turn, but I knew that whatever I was hearing, it was on the other side of this door. Too late to turn back now.

I grasped the handle and pulled, increasing the force I applied slowly until I was giving it about three and a half times what a normal man was capable of. That was when I felt the mechanism start to give way inside the door. I jiggled the handle until I felt something engage, then slowly, slowly turned it.

Bingo. That had been enough to bypass the card reader's lock.

I gently pulled the door open and checked for people before stepping inside.

There were lights affixed to the sides of the tunnel I had now entered, though none of them were particularly bright. Once inside, I realized there was even more noise coming from the end of it.

I muscled the door handle back into place before closing it. Good as new...maybe? Then I followed this new path, passing clearly marked restrooms for men and women as I did, until it opened into a dome-shaped room. This area was also dimly lit. Except for some neon lights here and there, the rest of the light

was centered on a circular ring surrounded by ropes in the middle of the room. Around it sat bleachers, all facing the ring.

A crowd of a few dozen spectators occupied the bleachers, eyes trained on a small, frail-looking little girl inside the ring.

Her eyes looked up at mine, as though she was the only one who had noticed me. When our eyes met, I heard the babbling once more.

CHAPTER 36

JAMES

Light streamed in through the big living room window in my apartment. The morning chill still clung to the floor, cutting through my socks. I shuffled quietly through the hallway, stopping as I spied Brandon at the kitchen table.

He suddenly stiffened. He was significantly more jumpy than I had remembered. I didn't know if that was because he didn't trust me, or if there was something else at play. I tried to put myself in his shoes and look at things from his perspective. If I hadn't seen someone in years, and all of a sudden they were hanging out with human-animal hybrids that I may or may not have known existed all of this time, I supposed I couldn't necessarily say how I would act or feel. To be honest, for better or worse, I'd probably just move on. Being friends with a hybrid, one who is the government's property—whether they were in possession of it or not—could only bring trouble.

I remembered that I was, in fact, also government property. And I had been even when I knew Brandon. All of the orphans in the United States were. All of the surrendered kids. I had always been government property, for as long as I could remember. And I supposed he had been as well. He just didn't know that I was a hybrid now, too.

Brandon's eyes slowly tracked to mine. He was deep in thought.

"Can we take a walk?" he asked.

"Sure," I shrugged.

I walked over to the door and unlatched the lock before opening it for him to step through. He nodded. There were little ways in which I could still see the Brandon I had known. From the slight tilt when he nodded to the way one side of his lip always stayed a little upturned. It was eerie seeing him all grown up now because when I wasn't looking, I still saw him as the kid I'd known. But neither of us were kids anymore. Much had changed. The world had changed. We had changed.

"This way is a little more off the beaten path." I hiked my thumb in the direction I had in mind.

He wordlessly followed, his eyes still swarming with unspoken thoughts.

Brandon seemed icier than the air itself, and I couldn't tell if he meant to be or not. In some ways, he reminded me of Adam. Very quiet and aloof. But he wasn't warm like Adam. As a kid, though, he had been an absolute clown. Always boisterous and making people laugh. I wondered what happened.

"Well," I said at length, shoving my hands in my pockets, "how have you been?"

It was stupid. But I couldn't think of anything else to say. I didn't know what he wanted. This wasn't exactly a class reunion type of catch-up, but I wished that it was.

He stared at me, his eyes hard and full of shadows. His jaw was tight and clenched.

"You scared me, you know that?"

That was not what I was expecting him to say.

"I finally made it to the compound and you were gone! Metal was melted like it was nothing. I nearly had a heart attack when I pulled those cameras! What did you do with that fire thing?"

I gulped. This was going to be a little bit difficult to explain.

"She's not like that all the time, I promise." Somehow, I felt like I was introducing a girlfriend to my parents. "She's actually really nice and usually not on fire."

Brandon's eyebrows shot up far enough that they might as well have flown off of his face.

He looked straight ahead, rubbing his right arm as though it was hurting him. I frowned.

"Maybe you should take things from the top," he suggested.

I truthfully didn't know what Titania would be comfortable with me sharing. Heck, I didn't know what *I* was comfortable sharing, either. It seemed that neither of us were who we had been when we had last seen each other. Could I trust him? Could he trust me?

"I need to know that you aren't going to turn her in," I said. After all, he had kidnapped Luna and Silen. Now that we didn't have Silen as a source of intelligence anymore, I had to admit that the girls had been right to keep him around, despite what a pain in the butt he had been.

But kidnapping didn't fit an innocent profile, even if he was just trying to save me from what he thought might be a monster.

Adam wasn't going to easily let go that Luna had been taken, either. We needed to establish where each other stood on some things before this went any further.

"As long as she's not a danger, I wouldn't do that," Brandon said.

"How do you decide whether or not she's a danger?" I probed. "She's not a danger to you and me, but if someone was trying to take her somewhere she didn't want to go, she might be a danger to them."

"How long have you known her?" Brandon countered.

"Long enough."

"And she's never done anything that caught you off guard? Never acted in a way that you weren't expecting?"

I bit the side of my lip. If catching on fire counted, then yes.

"Never kept secrets from you?" he went on. "How do you know that you know her?"

I did not like this line of inquiry. I could understand that he was suspicious, but this was Titania we were talking about. She had kept her true nature a secret from me to protect me. That wasn't malicious.

"How do I know that I know *you*?" I countered. "It's been some years."

"You don't," he said, his face expressionless. "That's my point."

I resolved to have him stay with me in the apartments. I didn't want him around the girls or the kids with his loyalties being in question.

"All I need to know about you right now is if you support what happened to her, the experimentation. Because if you do, then we need to part ways as old friends right here, right now.

But if you don't, then everything else can be discussed and worked through," I said simply.

His face turned ashen, as though he was recalling something that he didn't want to.

"I don't."

"You don't what?"

"I do not support the Titan project."

"Great," I said, secretly breathing a sigh of relief because it would hopefully make the idea that I was also a crazy animal-human hybrid much more palatable later.

"But," he added, immediately deflating me, "just because I don't like what's been done to them doesn't mean that I trust the Titans."

I looked up at the gray sky, clouds thickening over the city. If I had known that calling Brandon was going to be this complicated, I might never have done it.

CHAPTER 37

TITANIA

I had hoped to have an easy, stress-free reunion with James when he got back, but he seemed to be avoiding me since our initial greeting.

"Where's James?" I asked Jen after I returned to the underbelly of the gym. He hadn't been in any of the nooks and crannies, not even Adam's office. I hadn't seen hide nor hair of him, Luna, or Adam since right when they got back into town. I was, truthfully, a little offended.

"I don't know," Jen said noncommittally. "Haven't seen him. It was kind of a madhouse earlier. You know how riled up these kids get."

I did know. But I was still disappointed.

I grabbed my coat off one of the hangers drilled into the wall by the door and stepped out into the chilly outdoor air.

The days were getting shorter and shorter. It was barely five o'clock and already there was a dusky haze setting itself across the sky. I decided to go to the apartments. Maybe James was getting settled in there and freshening up. I couldn't wait to hear all of the adventures they had had. Though Jen had filled me in on the fact that they had lost Silen in the process. I wasn't sure how I felt about that. On the one hand, it would be a relief not to see Silen every day. I had to admit, my blood pressure spiked every time I saw his face. But on the other hand, he was on the loose. He knew where we were, and he could bring people to us. I doubted he would do that; he wouldn't get anywhere with this being a sanctuary city. Cassandra wouldn't let people take us like that.

Still, his whereabouts being unknown didn't sit well with me. I needed to talk to Luna about it. She seemed to be able to read people well. Sometimes boys just dismissed things, telling you what they think you want to hear. But I didn't want platitudes and consolation. I wanted to know the truth. How much of a danger did she think he was?

I'd have to knock on her door after I had a talk with James. After all that lovey-dovey stuff he said in his letters, I couldn't believe he wasn't chomping at the bit to see me.

Had something happened on the trip?

There were kids playing in the street as I approached the part of town that was inhabited. On the outskirts, there wasn't a lot of movement, so it was pretty safe for them to do that. One of them kicked a ball. It came flying right at my face. My hand shot up just in time to stop it, and I had to grit my teeth to keep from instinctively heating my hand up as though it were a threat. I didn't want to char their ball.

"Here you go!" I said as I tossed it back to them.

"Thanks, lady!" a little boy said through a thick lisp. I smiled, putting my hands in my pockets as I kept walking.

The apartment complex stairs felt as though they were about three times as long and four times as steep today for some reason. I would've taken the elevator, but it had been making a weird creaking sound that I wasn't a fan of. And it didn't sound like the landlord was particularly concerned about it, which didn't inspire confidence.

I stepped out onto our floor and padded across the concrete to James' door. No sooner than I lifted my hand to knock, the door cracked open just a smidge.

"James?" I asked. His eye went wide. It was the only thing I could see through the crack.

"I'll be out in a bit," he whispered.

I looked at him like he had grown two heads. "Is everything alright? Why are you whispering? What was the deal with that one guy last night?"

He looked even more frantic as he shooed me away and closed the door.

Anger flared in me. What was that about? I stuck around to find out.

Pressing my ear to the door, I listened for sounds. What was in there that he didn't want me to see? *Who* was in there? He hadn't picked up a new girlfriend, had he? As impractical and unlikely as that was, I was still overcome with jealousy.

He and someone else were talking low enough that I couldn't quite make out what was being said, but it was definitely a guy. And from what I could hear, it sounded like the guy who had been looking at me funny last night.

Whatever or whoever it was, I didn't like it. I had waited very patiently for James to come back. Stayed here like he had wanted me to. And now he had shut me out of his apartment and told me to shush!

I balled my fist and headed to Luna's apartment. Maybe she knew who this stranger was.

I knocked on Luna's door, reminding myself to cool my hand off before I did. Otherwise, I might singe her door. It was convenient for me to be able to warm myself up, but very inconvenient when I didn't remember that the rest of the world couldn't tolerate the heat that I could produce.

I listened for the sound of her rustling, but none came. I wondered if she and Adam were out decompressing from the journey. I seethed all over again that James wasn't answering the door. That should be us. I should've known that all that stuff he said in those letters I wouldn't get from him in person. He was too chicken to be that kind of vulnerable outside of me being dead, apparently. Either that or he had changed his mind. I didn't know which.

With no one to talk to, I decided to go on a walk myself. There was no point in sticking around, and I didn't really want to be around all of the kids and their high energy at this moment in time.

As I left, I wondered about Greg. Something inside me nudged me to go knock on his door. I hadn't ever checked on him before, but between the fire and his family's home being gone, I supposed he could use being checked on.

Impulsively, I walked over. The concrete flooring didn't disguise my footfalls in the least.

I knocked lightly. I didn't want to scare him. I wasn't sure that I'd ever witnessed anyone knock on his door before, and perhaps that would make him jumpy.

The creaking of a couch sounded from inside, followed by a faint whiff of cologne as the door cracked open.

"Hello?" Greg said, standing on the other side of the doorway. He looked…out of it.

"Hey, Greg," I said. "I just wanted to check on you after… everything. I know it's been a lot."

His usual chipper-ness wasn't there. The man had bags under his eyes so big that they looked like they could pull his whole face down if he let them. A frown etched itself onto my face, and I tried to smooth it out like a potter with clay.

"Oh, Titania," he said, slow to recognize me. "I'm sorry, come in, come in."

I halted. I hadn't anticipated being invited in, I just wanted to check on him. But I didn't want to be rude, so I accepted and stepped inside of the apartment. All of the units seemed to have roughly the same floor plan, with a few minor tweaks here and there. His reminded me of a cross between mine and Luna's, though the staple between all of them seemed to be the large windows that overlooked the city. Greg had flanked his windows with plants, which seemed fitting for him somehow. He seemed a man desperate to be at ease, without actually ever experiencing such a reality. A fake it 'til you make it sort.

"Have a seat." He motioned toward his couch.

There was a paper laid out across his coffee table with what I originally took to be a coffee stain on it. But upon sinking into his couch and catching a better glimpse, I found it was burned.

I withdrew my eyes in an instant, suddenly desperate to look at anything else. I stole a glance at him, busy pulling teacups down from out of the cupboard. Had he noticed me looking? I hoped not.

"How's your niece recovering?" I inquired. She had suffered some from the smoke inhalation. Even with my ability to set myself on fire and "reset" wounds, I could still feel parts of my throat that were raw. I couldn't imagine how it had been for her, with her being so tiny and in the thick of it.

"She'll make a full recovery," he said, pulling a tea kettle steaming with water off of the stove and pouring it into the two cups.

"Peppermint okay?" he asked, shifting his eyes to me.

"Yes, thank you," I said, though my stomach flopped. That was James' preferred tea. Some of the letters even smelled like it. I didn't want to think about that right now.

My eyes wandered the room. It was hard to believe beautiful places like this existed when I had grown up the way that I had. He had paintings hung on the wall, some of landscapes and others of birds.

I couldn't help but wonder how this could be so different from what I was used to. It seemed like the apocalypse of the nation was only felt by the poor or remote. And while I was sure that wasn't true, I couldn't help but shake the feeling that there was more to the story than what had been shown on TV as a kid. That maybe, for some people, the world went on as it always had, with minimal ramifications felt.

Greg's slacks swished as he crossed the room and took a seat with space in between us, his arm resting on the couch after he deposited the tea on the table, the tea bags bobbing up and down in the darkening liquid.

He'd set my cup dangerously close to that burned paper. I didn't dare reach for it. Any proximity to it felt as though it were a ticking time bomb about to go off. I knew he shouldn't have that. From the logo, I knew that it was something he was never meant to see. It was about the Titans. About people like me. And as much as I wanted to know what it said, I didn't want to open up that can of worms. Nothing good could come of Greg having this paper. I wondered if he already knew too much about me. But as I looked into his chocolate-colored eyes, I didn't see any indication that he saw me differently. I was the same old Titania to him. The quirky neighbor whose friends liked to cosplay.

"There is stuff going on that I'm not supposed to know about," Greg said, setting his tea down and picking up the paper. He licked his thumb, then flipped through the papers before setting them for me to see.

"But I think you know about them, don't you?" he asked. His voice held no accusation. Only sadness. "Cassandra pulled me into her office. She thought that I knew something about you that I wasn't supposed to. She was adamant."

The walls seemed to be getting closer and closer. I knew they weren't, but I couldn't shake the feeling. The one rule we had with Cassandra was to lay low. People weren't supposed to know what we were. Had I blown it when I saved his niece from the burning building? Had he ended up seeing something? Was that why she'd pulled him in, so she could question how much he had seen?

"I played dumb. I didn't know what she was talking about, but I could put the pieces together. I kept playing dumb though, don't worry," he reassured me, sinking into the couch. "Makes sense out of how you survived that burning building, though. Here you had me thinking I was inadequate for being unable to even be near the house without coughing my lungs out."

"I'm sorry," I said, though I wasn't sure what I was apologizing for. I just couldn't shake the sense that everything was about to change. That I had accidentally dragged him into something.

"Don't be," he said. "I understand why you didn't tell me. It sounds like nobody was supposed to know. But I love ya just the same. You're just Titania to me, regardless of what's going on."

"I guess she didn't believe you when you said you didn't know?" I ventured.

"Didn't seem to." He shook his head, then blew on his tea.

Hm. That maybe meant I needed to pay another visit to Cassandra. Just to smooth things over. Calm her down. Reassure her that nobody saw a thing.

"I'll talk to Cassandra next time I see her," I said, antsy. I wanted to get this over with. I stood. "Thank you for the tea."

"Of course, anytime." He nodded. "You be careful now. If you guys need anything at all, just holler."

"Thank you," I said. I couldn't picture calling Greg for help, but I hoped that it wouldn't even come up to begin with. I wasn't sure what kind of help Greg could even be. But the gesture was appreciated, nonetheless.

CHAPTER 38

ADAM

The next night, I was beneath the city again. I should've known better than to go back, but I couldn't help myself. Luna always said my greatest weakness was looking back over my shoulder. And that was probably true. I spent a lot of time…regretting the past. But if I didn't act in the present, it could become the past I regretted all over again. I couldn't just sit by and watch something terrible happen.

My head was never really clear, it was just slightly less loud. But tonight, it roared at a fever pitch tone that gave me a headache. There were too many thoughts and instincts rushing across my proverbial desk.

That little girl I had seen in the ring haunted me.

I hadn't heard the voice since last night, and I wondered if something had happened to her. Had it been her? I didn't want it to be true. If there was really another Titan in the city that we had no knowledge of, that could mean all sorts of bad things. I absolutely wanted all Titans to be free, but if others were escaping without a plan or guidance, they could blow the freedom that all of the rest of us had. We were only able to walk free without being hunted down if we hid in plain sight, if we acted like everyone else. The government could search for us all they wanted, but there was no way for them to track us outside of the trackers and eyewitness accounts. But some of these Titans were just kids. They were escaping and doing whatever they had to in order to survive, and for some that meant they were showing their transformations to people who were never supposed to have any knowledge of our existence.

The Titan program, even when it had been planned to be utilized, was always supposed to be something kept quiet. There were ways to fight with weapons that the general public had no knowledge of. It happened all the time. And if they were caught? Photoshop was always a good excuse. CGI. They had every opportunity to hide what they were doing. But rogue Titans threatened that opportunity.

I was worried about this little girl, about her safety. But I was worried about other Titans like her, too, off on their own.

I made it to the manhole, slipping in and descending the stairs. The noise was easy to follow again. It was amazing what could be hiding right under people's noses and they were never the wiser to it.

The tunnel's mustiness felt particularly oppressive this evening. I had to catch myself before I sneezed and gave away my position. I wanted to slip in quietly and observe for a while. Last time, I had chickened out and left before I felt like I could draw any lasting conclusions.

I'd learned that the best way to blend in in any situation was to be quiet and move silently.

Be completely forgettable.

But, if that didn't work, I always had plan *B*.

The door responded exactly as it had before, allowing me inside without whatever key card that seemed to usually be required. I found the dim dome room packed full of people again. There was popcorn skittering across the floor, drinks sloshing as people raised them and cheered, and a lot of hooping and hollering.

This was what happened when you took away people's ability to watch football, I thought. They would always find a way to have a spectator sport, even during the apocalypse.

I found a seat in the bleachers to my left without anyone else in it, but wedged between someone above, offset to the side, and someone below. With the lock on the door leading in, no one had any reason to suspect that I didn't belong there just as much as they did.

I watched as some men hauled off a teenage boy from the stage, his nose bloodied. His opponent, a teenage girl, walked away heaving and doubled over with exhaustion.

I tried to keep my brow from furrowing. Even if there were no Titans involved in this, this didn't seem like it was on the up-and-up.

No sooner had the thought crossed my mind than a familiar face was led out into the arena and left there.

The little girl locked eyes with me and, a moment later, I heard a weak jabbering. I still didn't know what she was saying. I wished that I did.

It occurred to me that maybe, if I got close enough to touch her and absorb her power, I could communicate with her. But I didn't want to blow my cover, or hers. I especially didn't want to jeopardize her safety.

From the other side of the arena, a grown man was led out and brought onto the fighting floor. My heart dropped into my feet. This was not a fair fight, surely everyone could see that!

And yet, not a single person said a word.

I sighed, shifting uncomfortably.

Patience, I told myself. I was here to gather information. I couldn't blow my cover as a Titan or as someone unsympathetic to this form of entertainment. Humans had a knack for finding exploitation most amusing.

But I couldn't help myself. My feet were walking me away from my seat and into the narrow way that led to the arena. I pretended to just be trying to find a better vantage point.

Inebriated people swayed around me as I made my way to the child. She seemed completely unconcerned with her much larger opponent.

In fact, she seemed distracted. She was looking directly at me. I looked away, hoping to persuade her to look at something else. I didn't want her to blow my cover. Even though she was the size of a six-year-old *maybe*, she acted and moved more like a clumsy toddler. I looked back at her as I got closer, and something stopped me in my tracks.

She had a unique-looking scar. That was…interesting. She reached her hand out to me without a care in the world. I still wasn't close enough to make contact, but it would only take a few seconds. If only I could get to her before the deranged-looking grown man who was circling her in the arena did. I wondered if Cassandra would be willing to bail me out of the mess I might be about to cause if I got in between these two.

Now or never. I grabbed onto one of the ropes that encircled the arena and hoisted myself up.

The man suddenly lunged and brought his hands down to hit the girl with what looked like full force. Before I could stop him, he made contact with her. But instead of her little body giving way, he was inexplicably blown back.

In that moment, I realized that this was much, much more complicated of a situation than I had initially thought. She was not human. And her handlers at the edge of the ring knew that.

And to top it off, they were not very happy about me being here.

"No interfering with the fight!" they screamed, spit flying as they moved to lay hands on me.

"Sorry," I said, though I was not in the least bit sorry.

I threw my hands up and stepped down from the ring. The girl had shown that she was safer than I'd thought. The urgency I felt before was not gone, but it had diminished.

"Round two!" called a male voice, blasting throughout the room through a loudspeaker. I closed my eyes as the fight started.

I might have to play the long game, but I was going to get this child out of here.

CHAPTER 39

JAMES

Brandon was a lot moodier than I remembered him being. I desperately needed some time to myself and, thankfully, he seemed to be prone to sleeping in.

I slipped out in the early morning hours and gently knocked on Titania's door. The scowl she gave me when it opened was enough to melt my eyebrows off, and she wasn't even ignited at the moment. Her hair was a mess from sleep, but mercifully free of flames.

I winced.

"I'm sorry," I said. "I can explain."

"Explain what?" she said, folding her arms in frustration. Her PJ shirt hung precariously off of one shoulder, but the cold air didn't seem to bother her at all. She didn't even seem to notice.

"Brandon is a little…"—how could I put this tactfully?—"skeptical, of all of this," I finished.

"I just want to make sure that everyone is safe and that he doesn't cause more problems."

"Brandon? As in, the guy you called for help when we were at Oak Hollow over a year ago? That's the sullen dude from the other night that you've been harboring in your apartment?" Titania was incredulous.

She looked even more displeased than she had been before.

"Yeah, it's complicated..." I started explaining.

"Why not just send him back wherever he came from?" she asked, as though he were a puppy or some kind of pet.

"I don't know that he can go back."

In fact, that was something I intended to ask him about when things settled down a little. I didn't know how much he may have given up to come and help me. He'd most assuredly had to sacrifice something. But, at the same time, he had the resources to help, so...I just wasn't sure. I didn't know if I fully trusted him.

She harrumphed.

"I'm sorry," I said, frowning. I didn't dare reach out to touch her.

"I'll make it up to you," I continued. "I promise."

She leaned against her door, looking thoughtful.

"How?" she asked.

"Hmmm," I said, contemplating my options. "How about a date? Just the two of us? There are plenty of places in the city we could go out to eat. It's not like we've ever been on a real date before."

I don't think that was the answer she was expecting. I saw the wheels turning in her head as she contemplated how much she still wanted to be mad at me, contrasting with how much she seemed to perk up at the idea.

"Okay," she said, reluctantly accepting this gesture, "but you better not chicken out on me."

She poked me in the chest.

That was the Titania I knew. And loved.

My lips pulled up into a smile. "Deal."

"Good," she said, "because I could easily turn you into *fried* chicken."

I laughed, a little too loudly. I forgot that I was trying to stay quiet.

I stole a glance at my apartment door, nervous to get back to what I hoped was a still-sleeping Brandon.

"Soon." I nodded at her as she closed the door.

I snuck back in to find Brandon sitting at the kitchen table, staring out bleary-eyed at the city.

His hand was wrapped around a steaming mug of tea. My eyebrows knit together as I got closer.

"Morning," I said, wondering how that wasn't hurting him to hang on to. I would expect something like this from Titania; nothing burned her.

"Morning," he said through a scratchy throat.

A glint of metal peeked out at me where his sleeve fell down, exposing his arm.

I looked away as he went to adjust it.

For a moment, I was able to successfully tell myself that it had been a watch. I didn't have any better explanation for it. But I knew that wasn't true. I just didn't know what *was* true.

His hand came away from the mug with not so much as a red mark on it.

Curious, I thought.

"How did you sleep?" I asked, trying to move things along in case he had caught me staring at him.

"Okay," he said, adjusting in his chair so that his body was facing me.

"Good."

I looked out over the city. The world had gotten so much bigger, and somehow smaller at the same time recently. It was surreal to have a childhood friend drinking tea in what we would've considered a fancy apartment when we were kids. Now I didn't know what he was to me, and I knew he felt the same. There was a lot of ground to cover between the two of us.

"So what happened?" I asked him, "After we went our separate ways."

He looked down into his mug, as though it had all the answers. Then he sighed.

"That's a great question."

CHAPTER 40

JAMES

"Did you know about the Titan program before her?" he asked.

Her being Titania.

"No," I answered truthfully. "Did you?"

His eyes shifted to anywhere but mine.

"Maybe."

I cocked my head to the side. "Maybe?"

What did that mean? How could you maybe know that the government was experimenting on children? Seemed like something that you were either all in or all out about when it came to the knowledge of. Especially considering what a closely guarded secret they tried to keep it from what I'd observed. Just because some people were sloppy didn't mean that the whole program was.

I couldn't read the expression on Brandon's face. It looked… almost *amused*. I was very, very confused. He picked his mug back up and blew on it, which again, should've burnt his hand.

"How is that not hurting you?" I asked incredulously.

He smiled.

"I may not have known about the Titan program, but I did know the government was experimenting on kids."

That did not answer my question at all. What was he on about?

He set the cup down calmly, watching for my reaction. When I just stared at him, dumbstruck, he continued.

"I hurt my arm after you left. An accident with a chain saw."

"Oh," I said, my brows knitting together. "I'm sorry."

Really, he was probably too young to be using a chain saw. But the government hadn't cared about child labor laws in a while, if they ever really had to begin with.

"They weren't able to save my arm," he said, rolling up his sleeve, "so they gave me a new one."

My eyes went as big as dinner plates as Brandon brandished a mostly metal arm up to the elbow. His hand looked like a completely normal human hand, but somewhere past his wrist it was just metal until it connected with real flesh.

I shuddered.

"That's wild, man," I said. "I'm glad you still have some kind of hand, at least?"

"Oh, I am, too…don't get me wrong. But this thing came at a cost."

My face dropped. "What do you mean? What kind of cost?"

He flexed his hand out in front of him, admiring the bionic contraption.

"What did they do to you?" My voice dropped low. I imagined what they had done to Titania. Heck, I remembered what they had done to me. I should've considered that whatever they did to him would've been similar. Just because it wasn't gene splicing didn't mean that it was painless or ethical in any way.

"You know how these things go; there is always a catch."

"So, what's the catch on this?"

"I don't know yet."

"That seems…"

"A little scary?"

"Yeah."

"It is," he affirmed. "I don't know what they have planned for it, and I know that I am not the only one that they did this to. So when you called and I found the footage with that girl, I didn't know what to think."

He sighed, leaning back into the couch.

"That's understandable."

"It's hard to know who to trust, James. Do you know how many people I had to vet to get the crew I had trying to find you? Everyone is a double agent out here."

That did not inspire confidence in me. Not only was I unsure about people in this situation to begin with, but I already had a healthy dose of paranoia and skepticism. I didn't really need more reasons not to trust people.

"Can they track you with that thing?" I asked him, staring at his arm.

That could be a problem. And Adam would *certainly* have a problem with it. But I wondered if it was something that Adam could disable. He'd done it for Titania, but that had been in her blood. I didn't know what this thing operated on.

"I don't know, but I expect so. But I haven't given them a reason to track me. They think I am investigating some kind of corruption right now. Auditing some employees. They have no idea what I'm actually doing."

"Well…" I gulped. "That's good, I suppose. Adam might be able to take a look."

"Not sure that Adam wants to help me." He rubbed the back of his neck.

I winced. "I'm sure we can smooth things over, eventually."

Though we might ought to give him a week, I thought. Some time to cool off and spend time with Luna with no interruptions or danger. We were all at our wits' end.

"For now," I said, leveling with him, "I just need you to be cool. These kids have been through a lot, which you would understand. I've been with them for a while, and I don't think they are a threat to us."

"While that may be true, you all being together might be a threat to yourself."

"What do you mean?" I asked.

"If I can find y'all, so can anyone else trying hard enough."

CHAPTER 41

ADAM

"What do you mean there is another Titan?" Luna said incredulously. We sat around Titania's kitchen table—James, Titania, Luna, and me.

I'd waited as long as I'd dared to bring everyone together over this, but I didn't want to let another day go by without letting them in on what I'd found. Luna was easy to round up, and this was Titania's place, but I'd had to send Titania after James since I was putting off dealing with Brandon any more than I had to.

"I swear to you," I said earnestly, hands open on the table, "I saw her with my own two eyes."

"What kind of Titan is she?" James asked.

"Like, what kind of animal?" Titania asked. Titania always had a particularly strong investment in knowing what type of animal other Titans were. That was because she wasn't an animal. She was a phoenix. And she always wanted to know if there were more like her.

I could understand that.

I was also curious what this little girl was.

"I don't know."

"How do you not know?" James asked. "You saw her, didn't you?"

"I saw her, but I didn't see her transform into anything. She did have a weird scar, but what was really weird is that she got hit and the other person went flying back."

Luna's eyebrows shot up. She'd seen enough weird things happen to know that this raised some questions. Titans, especially Titans that didn't know how to use their powers, always had the most random things happen that they couldn't control. Usually when they were under attack. Before Titania had her transformations under control, she was really only able to influence her powers if something was bearing down on her.

"So, what's the plan?" Luna asked, her leg bouncing nervously under the table. I was sure that her nerves were worn way too thin. She hadn't even had a real chance to recover from getting kidnapped and now we were on to the next thing. It seemed like everything was always breakneck speed for us.

"I don't have one," I admitted. I was spinning so many plates behind the scenes, it felt impossible to add another one.

"Maybe we should just watch and wait," I offered. "She's obviously lasted this long. Just keep assessing. She didn't seem to get hurt."

"Yeah, but..." Titania bit her lip. "If the people watching don't already know about Titans, the more she gets shown off like that, the more people are going to grow suspicious. It could cause a real problem for all of us, you know?"

I highly doubted anyone in this underground fighting ring was about to go blabbing about how they enjoyed seeing unusual little kids get beat up.

"I don't know that these folks are going around talking about it."

But, she had a point.

I buried my head in my hands. This was a disaster. Why did I have to hear her in the first place? We just needed to catch a break. How could we possibly get her out of there without making someone mad.

An idea came to my mind.

"I wonder if they'd sell her to me."

Three faces were aghast as they watched me from across the table.

That did, admittedly, sound bad. But I was trying to think of ways that would make sense in this context and wouldn't raise any red flags with the organizers.

I was running on fumes from back-to-back trips and little sleep. I just needed ideas.

There was not a doubt in my mind that this…this was a bad idea. Going by myself was one thing. I could blend in. Literally, that was what I was made for. But the others… Well, they wanted to see, and if we were going to get this girl out of here, I needed their help.

I looked around, surveying them as they noisily walked behind me. Getting us all down the manhole had been a feat in and of itself. Luna knew the drill. Quiet. Stealthy.

But James and Titania hadn't quite come into their own yet. They weren't as adept at sneaking and not attracting attention to themselves. They also were a little more grossed out by the sewage that surrounded us. Particularly James. I supposed that made sense, given his former profession as a medic. This wasn't the place to be if you wanted to avoid germs.

But they insisted. So here the four of us were, wandering the empty walkway of the underground Reunion City. I wondered how we were all going to get into the fight arena without being conspicuous. I'd tried to tell them that we should just add one person at a time, but once the cat was out of the bag, they were all impatient to see this little girl that I had told them about. My only saving grace was that I had been able to keep them at bay while I tried to figure out the schedule I heard her voice on.

I wasn't sure if she only called when she was in the fighting ring, or if she just babbled all of the time.

I still didn't know what language she spoke, and because I hadn't touched her, I couldn't understand what she was saying. And I couldn't communicate back to her yet. There was a notebook sitting in my office of frantically scribbled notes as I tried to document everything I could about this new person. Eventually, I'd be able to talk back to her in a way that she would easily understand.

Titania clung to James as I opened the door.

"How about you two stay out here?" I offered. At least that way, it would only be one extra person walking into the viewing area tonight.

James looked on board with this, but Titania scowled. There was a strange tension between the two of them that I couldn't make out. I hoped they could put it aside for now.

"Just for right now?" I requested patiently.

She reluctantly agreed.

Luna and I were practiced in silent communication. We could anticipate each other's moves, play off of each other with ease, and we knew how each other thought. James and Titania were wild cards. Once we all had a common way of operating, it would be easier to interchangeably operate and go in together. But for this, Luna was my best bet.

She and I took turns on who had the bleeding heart for Titan children. Today, it was me. She'd be able to more adequately assess the risk this little girl was in and come up with a better plan for how to get her out of here without ruffling too many feathers.

The arena was bustling, as always. I still couldn't believe that this couldn't be heard from the street. I had to remind myself that normal humans did not have the hearing that we all did. But even then, I hadn't noticed all the noise until I was tracking the little girl. And these folks certainly were not doing anything to keep it down. At this volume, there was either some kind of soundproofing involved, or we were further underground than I thought.

Luna followed me as I took a seat on the bleachers to the left again, this time with her plopping down right beside me. We were settling in, waiting for the little girl to appear, when something caught my eye from across the room.

A familiar face, chatting with a man to the left of her.

Cassandra.

My mind took off in a sprint.

What was she doing here? Did she condone this? She looked perfectly at ease, without a care in the world. She was laughing with the man next to her, her head thrown back.

Luna must've felt my muscles tense. She immediately clocked that I had found something, and when she followed my gaze to Cassandra, she hissed under her breath.

"This isn't good," she said.

"No," I moaned. "No, it most certainly isn't."

I debated. If we left, it might be more noticeable right now. But until we knew what was going on, I did not want Cassandra to see us here. That would not be good. I couldn't think of a single valid reason why she might be down here that would work in our favor.

Had she already looked this way? Had she already noticed me on another night, when I didn't notice her? I couldn't imagine that was the case. I was usually pretty observant.

"Let's go," I whispered to Luna, who was already carefully removing herself from the bleachers and making her way to the exit.

I was glad we had left James and Titania in the hallway.

I tried to keep an eye on Cassandra, as much as I could while walking away, until we were on the outside of the arena area.

"That was quick," James said.

Luna shot him a glare, raising her finger to her lip.

Titania's eyes went wide.

"What happened in there?" she asked anxiously.

"We'll fill you in later. Cassandra is in there, we need to go," I said, herding them toward the exit.

The sooner we were out of here, the better.

I had to think in a place that was far less noisy than this one.

A voice tugged at my heartstrings as we climbed back up the ladder. The little girl was going on.

I tried to strain my ears to see if I could hear Cassandra still in there, but I couldn't tell.

I still hadn't gotten a chance to touch her. My heart sank as I listened yet again to babbling that I couldn't understand.

Next time, I'd need an actual plan.

Next time, I'd save her.

CHAPTER 42

TITANIA

The darkness floated around me like wispy clouds. I reached out to touch it, and it didn't shy away from my hand, but wrapped around it like it was embracing me.

I shuddered involuntarily, trying to get the strange sensation to leave me. The hot, sharp pain of ice wound its way into every piece of skin it touched.

A voice called out to me, but when I turned, I saw nothing. There was no one there, just the darkness.

As it spoke, I realized it was the darkness that was talking.

"Don't worry," it said in a low, soothing tone. "I'm not here to take you again. Not yet. What a specimen you are…"

I frowned, wrapping my arms around myself.

"We will meet many times, Titania—or do you prefer Sam?" the voice said. "But don't worry, only for a time. Always, ever, only for a time."

I tried to run, but my legs wouldn't carry me. I tried to scream, but my voice came out empty and soundless.

Terror overtook me, until the next thing I saw was the ceiling of my bedroom.

A nightmare.

Another nightmare.

Every nightmare was stranger than the last.

I wished more than anything in the world that James were here. I knew that if he were, he would be able to fix it. He would be able to make the awful feeling go away. I pushed my fingers into my own skin, hard, desperate to scrape away the lingering sensation of ice burning me.

But James wasn't here. He was gone. Off with Brandon, probably. Adam's meeting that he had called at my place had been so awkward. I'd barely seen James, and trying to interact with him when I was still upset without the others seeing it was difficult.

My feet met the floor and, somehow, the sensation of being unable to move still clung to them. As though the darkness still had hold of me, pinning me in place.

I forced myself to move. Told myself that I just needed food. Grogginess clung to me, as it always did after a night of restlessness like that. I couldn't shake it, even with a warm meal or hot drink.

I reached up, opened my cabinet door and pulled out a box of cereal. I haphazardly poured it into a bowl, leaving it dry. I didn't care for soggy cereal, and I was not going to be eating anything fast right now.

No sooner had I sat down with my breakfast, curled up in a position that couldn't be good for my spine, than I heard a knock at the door.

It startled me, causing me to fumble with the bowl of cereal. Thankfully, there were only a few casualties that I could sweep up later.

I hurried to the door, curious as to who it could be. I half expected it to be Greg, returning the drop-in visit I had paid him earlier. My face froze when James stood in my doorway, as handsome as ever. His light eyes and dark skin were a lethal combination. My oasis in the desert.

"Good morning." He smiled.

"Morning," I managed as I stepped out of the way, cursing myself for not having brushed my hair yet. I probably looked a mess.

I sighed, deciding that I didn't want to know.

I began nervously running my fingers through my hair, trying to get out any of the tangles that I could.

He loitered between my kitchen and living room, clearly unsure where to go or what to do.

"I was wondering if we could talk," he asked, looking down at me through thick eyelashes.

I wondered if this was about him blowing me off because of Brandon the other day. I was trying to be get over that.

"Sure," I said, taking a seat with my cereal on the couch again. I took a bite of it and recognized very quickly how much of a mistake that had been. Between James being here and the lack of moisture in the cereal, my throat was suddenly very, very dry.

I could feel a cough coming for me. My eyes teared up as I struggled to keep it at bay. James, ever a man, was entirely oblivious to my plight. Just as well, I thought, as I chewed and tried to pay attention.

"I just wanted to apologize for the other day," he said, motioning in the direction of his apartment. "I've worked things out with Brandon and I don't think he's going to cause any issues. But it got me thinking."

"About what?" I asked, trying to be nonchalant. The longer he sat there, the more I could smell the peppermint from his morning tea and the natural scent of the woods that he always seemed to have. It was more pronounced now that he was a Titan, too. I didn't know how that worked. It seemed like, sometimes, being spliced with something else made us into even more intense versions of ourselves.

"I've just been thinking about…" he paused, his face reddening, "…about us. And I don't see things slowing down anytime soon. I still haven't given up on finding a cure, but I do think we need to be prepared for things to stay as they are. That we might both be stuck like this forever."

"Okay…" I said hesitantly, nervous about where he was going with this.

"I'd like to figure out a new normal. I don't want everything to constantly get in between us." He turned toward me as he spoke. "I want you. I don't want anything standing in the way."

Now it was my turn to turn red. This was the James who wrote those letters. I wondered what was causing him to be so bold this morning.

My brain screamed and panicked until I realized that he was waiting for me to respond.

"Um," I said. Then I mentally kicked myself. He eagerly awaited what I had to say and I had absolutely nothing eloquent to add.

"Sorry," I said. "My brain is a working a little slow. I've been having nightmares. I'm still waking up." I motioned to my head.

"Nightmares?" He frowned, scooting closer to me and enveloping me in his arms.

Quite forward.

I…didn't hate it. I wasn't going to tell him that, though. I awkwardly leaned into him, my pulse shooting through the roof. I had to remind myself not to roast him like a marshmallow since my body's first instinct was to be flammable at the hint of any emotion.

"Yeah," I said, trying to remember how to form words. "Just the usual. Scary, dark, weird."

"Tell me about it." I felt him say it more than I heard it, with his chest pressing against my arm and his head so near to my ear.

"There's just this weird darkness." I threw my hand up in exasperation. "And apparently it's learned to talk. It didn't used to talk."

I sounded insane. I knew it. But to be fair, everything about the situation was insane. I had died. Literally. Gone for a whole year. Life had moved on without me. I didn't know that I was coming back. Neither did anyone else. In case you didn't know, dying is a little traumatic. And resurrecting a year later, while very helpful and I wasn't complaining about it, was also traumatic.

"What did it say?" he asked, and I was surprised when his tone didn't have a hint of teasing or incredulity, just concern.

"It said something about it would see me again but it would never keep me. Maybe I need a shrink." I laughed, but it wasn't funny. I didn't like it and I wanted it to stop.

"Wow," he said. "It sounds a little deranged."

"You could say that," I grumbled.

"Maybe you just need some time to relax," James offered, his brow furrowed. "To get your mind off things. It hasn't been that long, and I think this would weigh on anyone."

"Maybe so."

"How about we go on that date?" he said.

"Date?" I blinked. That rang a bell.

It felt weird to think about going on a date. We hadn't had that option in the compound, *or* while on the run, really. And we'd been a little busy rescuing people as of late. It didn't occur to me to do things like go on dates since we'd been in survival mode so often. But there were plenty of places in the city where a person could go on a date.

I recalled watching the TV as a kid and seeing people go on dates.

"Yeah," James said. "Why not? We could go out to eat together, just sit and talk. Pretend we're not animal-human hybrids for a bit."

"That sounds nice," I admitted.

"Great. I'll pick you up at six p.m.?" he asked, rubbing my arm. I could've fallen right back to sleep with him doing that, but I forced myself to stay awake. It did chase away the pain, though.

"Okay," I agreed, trying not to get my hopes up too much. Something always happened to ruin things. But I wanted to at least try.

"I've got some things to tend to," James said, standing up and taking my hand before giving it a light squeeze. "I'll see you later."

"See you later," I said, watching as he walked to my door.

The second it closed, I gasped.

If I was going to go on a date, I would need something to wear.

I bounded off the couch, in pursuit of some real clothes out of the money from the small allowance we got from Cassandra.

I wasn't sure what we were going to do about that whole situation with her and the underground, but it wasn't a problem for tonight. Tonight, I had a date!

CHAPTER 43

TITAN ON THE LOOSE

A boy with hair in his eyes trudged through the woods.

He was haggard and caked with dirt. He was still fighting the effects of a tranquilizer. He wasn't sure if he'd win the battle or succumb.

He had to keep moving.

A pang of sorrow overwhelmed him as he considered what would happen if the place he'd heard rumor of really existed. If he made it all this way to succeed when everyone else had died…

His heart pounded more with every step. What if they weren't there anymore? What if he made it all this way to fall back into the hands of mad scientists? If he were a cat, he would've guessed he was almost out of his nine lives.

He broke through the trees and rushed into the city. He kept his head down, not making eye contact with anyone. The less attention he drew to himself the better. He twisted and turned through the streets, the traffic lessening and lessening. They wouldn't be in a busy part of town, he knew. They'd be laying low. At least, if they were smart. And to make it this far out of a facility, they had to be.

That, or crazy.

He looked for signs of life in the haunted part of town. They likely wouldn't be somewhere totally dilapidated, with broken windows or doors that hung off the hinges. That didn't leave many spots. Maybe this was a dead end. His head throbbed from fighting the tranq, and his vision reddened. If he just sat down and rested for a moment…yeah, that was all he needed. He sank to his knees.

His consciousness began to slip, whether it was from the exhaustion or the tranquilizer, he couldn't say. Caught between wakefulness and nightmare-inducing memories, he found himself re-living the events that had brought him here.

A guard slipped a key into the lock of a cage. A cage far too small for a human. But a human was held inside of it anyway.

You'd think that would be a relief, to be able to stretch out and take a full breath. It was never a good thing when they unlocked our cages. The person never came back. He used to wish they'd unlock his cage. He used to be happy for the people that got let out.

Then one of his friends, Daniel, was let out. He could still feel the ice in the room when he thought about Daniel taking some of his last steps. Had he fought? He couldn't tell. He'd never heard the clattering when anyone else had been let out. Or the bloodcurdling scream.

He hadn't known for sure what had happened, until one day they'd gotten a young, talkative guard. They'd heard all sorts of things between him and the people he talked to on the radio. He was just a kid, like everyone there was, but he was free.

He told one of his friends about the culling. He'd thought all the Titans were asleep. All of the guards thought that the Titans slept more than they did. The boy had insomnia, but was good at faking it. Whatever they had injected him with was something that didn't need much sleep, because it was worse than it ever had been for him.

He'd learned through the radio conversations that other people turned into the animals they were spliced with. None of this group had, and nobody knew why. They didn't tell him and his comrades what they were spliced with. Maybe they were failed experiments. Maybe that's why they were being culled.

Some of his friends had claustrophobia so badly that they'd panic 'til they passed out and then would do it all over again when they woke up. Right now, the guard was the only one who was awake and talking. Not having anyone to talk to and being awake so much was a prison all its own.

The guard talked about all sorts of things with his friend. Mostly girls, though. Occasionally there was excitement over news within the system. Like one day, some Titans just disappeared from a facility. At shift change, an incoming guard found all the other guards tied up or knocked out.

He could tell it made the guard uneasy. And it should have. Because it planted a seed in the boy's mind.

If other Titans could escape, they could, too.

CHAPTER 44

TITANIA

Not once had shopping for dresses been on my list of to-dos in my life. If I had gone dress shopping with my mother while she wasn't on a bender, I certainly didn't remember it. I did remember commercials for clothing stores and malls, and mail catalogs with clothes in them. I wondered if they still had those? I wondered if there were more cities like this one, maybe plenty more. My hopes lifted, like I was flying on the wind. James and I could travel, if that were the case. If we could go from sanctuary city to sanctuary city, we could see the world. Of course, it would take us ages to see everything that this one had to offer. But the prospect of the world being bigger and more interesting than it ever had been sent a thrill through my body. I involuntarily shook, trying to process it.

I wondered if I should invite Luna on this outing, but I decided I would actually prefer her help getting ready later. And she and Adam were catching up anyway. I knew that I had seen a dress shop downtown, I just couldn't remember exactly where.

But I wandered unhurriedly through the streets on the lookout for it.

I was beginning to recognize the people that typically lined the streets, and as it turned out, they were starting to recognize me, too. A few of them gave a little wave.

After a bit of wandering, I spotted the familiar storefront with dresses behind the glass.

I paused for a moment. It didn't feel like I should be the type of person to be wandering a dress shop. I was so used to everything being life or death, serious and intense. Dress shopping was an activity for someone who wasn't a science experiment gone wrong.

But I stuffed down the feelings, as heavy as they might be, and took a step forward. The only way to get over it was to go full steam ahead. If James wanted to try normal, I wanted to try normal, too.

A bell rang as I stepped through the door. The shop was a little sparse compared to what I was expecting, but every single dress looked like it may have been sewn by hand. Some of them had beautiful beadwork, tulle layered across bodices, and all sorts of other little touches.

I spun around, taking it all in as I looked around.

A woman called to me from behind the counter, "Let me know if you need anything."

I stopped, suddenly self-conscious.

"I will," I squeaked.

I tried to focus. What sort of dress would James like? There were some brightly colored ones, but when I held up my arm next to them, they made my olive-toned skin look sickly. That nixed the orange, the yellow, and a few other of the options that I liked. I kept looking.

A black dress hung on a mannequin to the far left of the store, all the way in the back. Something about it drew me in. Wasn't black supposed to be flattering on everyone?

I made my way to it, taking the fabric in my hand. It was soft, not too scratchy. The sides had cutouts, but they weren't overly scandalous.

"You can try it on if you'd like," the lady said, her voice startling me as she stood behind me.

"Oh," I said. "Okay."

She awkwardly removed the dress from the mannequin, keys jiggling on her wrist.

Then she led me to a door in the back, unlocking it and handing me the dress with a smile.

I blinked, holding it in my hands. It felt so bizarre to shuck my hoodie and worn-out jeans for a fancy dress like this, but when I turned and caught a glimpse in the mirror of the little closet-like dressing room, I knew this was the one.

It fit like a glove. Like it was made for me. I was reminded that I needed to ask Adam to fix up my protective suit. If there was one piece of clothing I did not want to lose to catching it on fire, it was going to be this dress. And not just because of the price tag.

I checked the time. I needed to get home quick to get ready for this date. I changed back, taking the dress to the counter to pay. The woman grinned at me while I dug out some cash from the allowance Cassandra gave me. "What's the special occasion, if I might ask?"

"A date." I smiled, feeling silly. Maybe people didn't usually buy fancy dresses for dates. But when a date was a special occasion, it seemed fitting.

"I hope it's a good one," she said, wrapping it up and handing me the bag.

"Thanks," I said, not able to contain my own stupid smile. "Me too."

CHAPTER 46

JAMES

I wasn't expecting to be as nervous as I was about this date. In some part of my mind, when I was thinking too deeply, Titania was still dead. I was still in terror every waking and sleeping moment. My muscles were all still tense, my eyes constantly leaking, and my head and heart aching.

I hadn't yet been able to fully get on board with her being alive again. Sure, I hadn't been anticipating it, so I hadn't planned on it. Not every guy expects his girl to be a phoenix, you know? But I was relieved, really. I just had a hard time accepting the reality.

We'd never gone on a date. What did I know about dates? We'd always just walked around at the compound, or outside. That was as exciting as things got, outside of our legendary card games.

But this…this was different. We were getting older. Things were more serious. I really needed to step it up.

I went downtown, stopping in at a few restaurants to see if I wanted to bring Titania later. I didn't know all of the rules about restaurants, so I was glad that I went. Most of them required a reservation. I made one at an Italian restaurant. Titania had always liked spaghetti at the compound, even if the meatballs weren't made of real meat. Not that she didn't have a hand in how they were made, working in the plant area there. But I remembered her always being excited about spaghetti.

I hoped that death hadn't changed her appetite. Her nightmare worried me a little. I wasn't sure what to make of it. She had been having a lot of them since the incident. I had been, too, of course, but I hadn't been the one who died.

I stepped inside a shop for men's clothing as I mulled over how I could help alleviate her anxiety about her nightmares.

A short man greeted me almost as soon as I walked through the door.

"How can I help you?" he asked excitedly.

I wondered if perhaps business was not booming. Either that, or he just didn't want me getting my grubby hands all over the nice clothes in here.

"I was wanting to get something nice for a special occasion."

I couldn't bring myself to say that it was a date. It felt like our evening could be jinxed over any little thing. Something was always going wrong, and I wanted this to be completely perfect.

The man sized me up, his hand wrapping around his chin as he looked me up and down. It was a bit comical as he was quite a bit shorter than me.

"Follow me," he said, guiding me through the racks of clothing.

He became a human whirlwind, pulling things off their hangers and shoving them into my hands before reaching out for my ear and dragging me to a place to change.

I barely had time to catch my breath before I found myself in a small room with poor lighting. I shimmied out of my clothes and into the ones he had selected for me. I could only hope that he had good taste. I wasn't sure that I did.

I emerged from my cave with the outfit on. He spun his finger in a circle, indicating I should turn around.

The man tsked beneath his breath. That seemed like a bad thing.

He flew off, leaving me standing awkwardly in the middle of the store as he tore through it in search of acceptable replacements for what I was wearing. I once again was thrown back into the small room to change.

We repeated this song and dance until he declared that what I had on was acceptable enough, he guessed. It felt a bit big, but after the ordeal I had just gone through, I didn't want to argue with him.

"Just bring it back in a few days," he said, as he mounted a stool behind the checkout counter, and his fingers began flying over the keys, inputting numbers.

"Bring it back?" I asked.

"Yes," he said irritably. "It's a rental."

He looked up at me through the top of his glasses.

"I don't suppose you wanted to pay for it outright?"

I heard the implication. He didn't think I could afford it.

"Rental is great," I said. "I'll have it back exactly the way it is now."

I would be careful. I was always careful.

"I'm sure you will," he said as he put the pieces into a garment bag and handed them to me, along with my change.

I'd have to be extra mindful about that spaghetti sauce, I told myself. But it would be worth it. I couldn't wait to see Titania's reaction to the outfit. I didn't know if she'd care, but I had a suspicion that she'd find it interesting. Even if it was just her swatting me on the shoulder for being too fancy.

Gosh. I had missed her swatting me on the shoulder.

CHAPTER 45

TITANIA

"You want me to what?" Luna asked incredulously as I stood at her doorstep.

A handful of lemon halves lay on her counter, along with a pitcher. She seemed to be in the middle of making homemade lemonade. I was always surprised by her ability to maintain monotony and peace when there was so much going on. She seemed to be able to believe in slowing down and having some kind of normal life.

"I want you to help me get ready for a date," I said, opening the bag to reveal the dress I had picked out at the store.

"I'm not sure I'm the best person for that…" Luna looked antsy.

"I'd say you're better than Jen probably is."

Luna tilted her head back and forth. "That's probably true…" then added reluctantly, "I'll be over in five minutes."

"Sounds good."

I had never been so sweaty in my entire life.

Not while being transformed into a freak of nature.

Not while escaping, running for my life the many times I had.

Not while fighting or training.

Never.

And James was going to be here ANY MINUTE.

"Calm down," Luna hissed as she brushed my hair.

She was sisterly, in her own way. She'd insisted on braiding my hair. She knew how much it liked to tangle and how little I noticed. This way it was at least out of my face. She braided it to flow down behind my back in little curly pieces. She held hair ties in between her teeth, my hair in one hand, and maneuvered my head in the other.

"I am nervous," I told her.

"I can see that."

"What if it doesn't go well? What if something happens?" I catastrophized. "Something ALWAYS happens!"

"What if the thing that happens tonight is that nothing bad happens?" she countered.

I was surprised at this bit of optimism from her.

"What if he doesn't like the dress?" I tried to angle myself to make eye contact with her.

She shoved my head back into place without a second thought.

"He'll love it."

"How do you know?" I protested.

"I know how boys are. They like dresses."

"But you've never worn a dress, least of all in front of Adam," I said.

At least, not that I had seen.

"Doesn't change the fact that he'd love it if I did."

"Hmm." I crossed my arms, considering this.

A knock at the door sent me flying into the air from my seated position.

Luna huffed, stalking over to the door.

"She's not ready yet; give us a few minutes," I heard her relay.

She came back, a smirk on her face.

My eyes went wide. "What?"

"Nothing," she said, all too quickly, before yanking on my hair again. "Just hold still."

I did as she asked, my heart beating out of my chest.

She declared that she was done, shooing me off to the bathroom to check her handiwork and freshen up.

The girl in the mirror was unrecognizable to me, even more so than when I had tried on the dress in the changing room. But it stirred up an unfamiliar emotion, one that I decided wasn't bad. It was just…different.

I stepped out. "Thank you for the help."

"Of course," she said, still giving me a coy look. "Now go. Romeo awaits. I'll clean up."

She motioned to the mess we'd made getting ready.

"Thanks," I said, carrying myself and my shaking hands to the front door.

The knob felt slippery as I turned it and opened the door. I almost closed my eyes. The sensation of lightheadedness was so strong, I could barely stand it.

James stood in front of me, a bouquet of flowers in his hands. He'd gotten a suit that was arguably just a touch too big, styled his hair, and stood as nearly unrecognizable as I was to myself.

"Hey," I said.

Stupid.

Stupid.

Stupid.

I couldn't come up with anything better than that to say?

My tongue felt like it was tripping in a desert full of sand or running through water.

"Hey," he said back, his eyes scanning me up and down. "You look…"

"Ridiculous," I said. "I know."

I was suddenly very self-conscious.

"I was going to say beautiful." His eyebrow twitched with amusement.

He extended the flowers to me, and I took the bouquet as if it were a hot potato. I had no idea what to do with them. Luna, thankfully, had still been hovering in the background. She found a jug that was tall enough to put them in and began filling it with water.

I mouthed *Thank you*, which she waved off, just like she had all of her other help.

"You two have fun," she said as she took the flowers and sent me on my way.

"Thanks," James said, waving to her.

He looked so happy. I couldn't remember the last time I had seen him so carefree. It had to have been before we left the compound. Maybe during one of our walks, just talking. I missed just talking. Missed solving all of the world problems from the confines of the building and surrounding woods. I couldn't believe this was where we had found ourselves. Being confined could be its own kind of freedom. Your problems were just as confined as you were. But being free meant that your ability to handle bigger problems was allowed to be infinite as well.

We'd come a long way.

I found myself staring at the way his hair curled into his temples, and the way his eyes shimmered in the evening light as we walked. He was truly a magical human being. Or, Titan, I supposed.

"May I?" he asked, extending a hand to me.

I stared at it like I hadn't ever seen a hand before. Then I watched as though someone else was operating my body, my own hand intertwining with his.

The warmth and happiness nearly knocked me out. The last time we had really held hands and had any kind of extended time to ourselves, he'd had to wear those welding gloves. I hadn't had enough time to really contemplate the fact that I had come so far in controlling my powers. That there was little standing in the way of us being able to have a relationship like we had always wanted to. The secret was out. The obstacle was gone.

But my fear was still there. The only solace I had was the fact that he had been spliced, too; that he understood what it was like to feel like something else, something *other*.

He could barely contain his upturned lip as we walked.

I squeezed his hand, nervous. He had always been my rock. Always been the person I could lean on, even when I couldn't tell him the truth about what I was.

"What do we do now?" I asked.

I had no idea. I felt like a dog that had caught up to something it was catching, having never anticipated actually catching it.

"I figured we'd go eat at the Italian place on the corner," James offered.

But I hadn't been talking about our date. I meant…*generally* speaking.

CHAPTER 47

TITANIA

James' suit coat was long enough that it covered his hand as we walked, which was just as well because it kept us both warmer on our way to the restaurant without me having to intervene.

Walking down the street together felt so strange. It wasn't that long ago that we had to hide how much time we were spending together at the compound. But, ultimately, nobody ever really put up much of a fuss. We were inseparable.

Still, this was new and different. I couldn't help but succumb to the butterflies that lightly danced in my stomach. I was thankful I could feel them now without setting my skin on literal fire.

The night air was briskly invigorating our lungs, but we still managed to carry on some semblance of a conversation.

"Do you think Luna and Adam are, like, *serious*?" I asked him, our intertwined hands swinging together.

I was genuinely curious. We hadn't seen a lot of relationships at the compound; it was kind of discouraged. But they did happen. I didn't have enough people to observe to really know what to think or figure out what I was looking at. They perplexed me, though, and I wondered if they left the same impression on James.

"They do seem to be, don't they?" His breath was smoke in the night air. His cheeks were flushed red from the cold. I wished I could reach up and touch them to warm them up, but I held myself back. I was too embarrassed.

"Yeah," I said. "There seems to be more there than we can see on the surface."

"They probably feel the same about us," James said, setting his green eyes on me.

Warmth suddenly hit me like a tidal wave. That was probably true, and I didn't know how to feel about it except embarrassed.

My mind wandered to something else.

I wanted to ask James about the time I had been away. About what he had done, besides moping, of course. But I didn't want to spoil the mood. I was also curious about his conversations with Brandon, though I set that curiosity to the side for the time being, too.

James led us down the street to a restaurant I hadn't ever noticed before. It came up so quickly, I didn't have time to hype myself up to ask him anything else.

We stepped up onto the sidewalk and under the awning. He opened the door and the smell of the food hit us immediately.

"After you." He motioned me through the doorway.

The place was lit with a warm, candlelight glow. While there were fancy chandeliers, they were dimmed. It stirred an emotion within me. Trepidation, maybe? This felt very serious and I wasn't sure that I could match that energy.

James seemed to put on a more professional air as a woman walked up to us, menus in hand.

"Reservation or Haven Club?" she asked brightly.

"Reservation," James confirmed, then made quick work of rattling off his name and all of the information she needed. I had to admit, I zoned out a little from overwhelm as they were talking.

My brain clocked back in from autopilot mode as she walked us toward the back of the restaurant.

She sat us at a booth, James facing me as we both slipped into the seats. She placed the menus in front of us and asked what we wanted to drink.

It was all a blur of talking and pleasantries, which I was not at all accustomed to.

I held the menu nervously as she clicked her pen, placing it and a notepad into an apron and scurrying away.

James seemed oblivious to my nervousness, which was good. Maybe by the time he was finished looking at the menu, I would have successfully collected myself. A girl could dream, couldn't she?

And in the process of fake perusing the menu, I noticed that there were actually a lot of things that sounded really good.

"Ooh, there is spaghetti!" I said excitedly, before I considered the serious atmosphere and tone of the place.

I shrunk into myself a little.

"I figured you would like that," James said, eyes peeking out at me over the top of the menu. "I remembered you liked spaghetti."

I paused. Had I ever told him that outright? I didn't think I had. He must've just noticed.

"Thank you," I said. That was very thoughtful of him. I didn't know what everyone else had eaten while I was dead, but I had been subsisting on little more than noodles, cereal, and other easily opened or warmed canned and pantry goods. Probably not a balanced diet but I was fine. I was very excited to be eating some real food cooked by someone else. That was something I really missed about living in the compound. One of the few things.

"What are you going to get?" I asked him out of curiosity.

"Probably the same thing you do," he said with a smile. "I'm not too picky. Food is food."

I smiled. He was a guy for sure. Weren't they all just bottomless pits? Except...

"Says the man who doesn't like Spam..."

"That's different," he started to protest, but he knew I had him dead to rights on that one.

The waitress interrupted us by bringing our waters and setting them down in front of us. The outside of the glasses were covered with condensation. She readied her clicky pen again.

"Ready to order?" she asked.

James answered for us. "I think we'll both have spaghetti and meatballs."

CHAPTER 48

TYLER

Not once had anyone ever knocked on my door. My one-bedroom apartment didn't get visitors. While it wasn't in a bad part of town, it wasn't in the best part of town either. And it was currently after dark.

I inhaled a steady breath, surveying my options. If the yellow-tinted kitchen light above my sink hadn't been on, I could've pretended I wasn't home. But the small window below it was perfectly illuminated, giving a clear view into my apartment, with me sitting at the kitchen table. I had been writing things down. I hadn't gotten to do that in what seemed like forever, but I liked to document what was going on, with dates and times. I didn't know who I ever thought would read it. It wasn't like I had a family coming to look for me or friends who knew where I was. Still, I couldn't shake the instinct to document everything I was seeing, despite the feeling that anyone who read it would think I was crazy.

Now, I was regretting that I couldn't inconspicuously stash the pencil and papers.

Another knock, this time far angrier, echoed through the thin walls.

I stood, wishing that I had a stronger weapon than a single shot of tranquilizer and a stun gun.

Closing the short distance between myself and the door, I looked through the dirty peephole. Seeing nothing, I quietly began retreating to the right, out of the line of sight of the window. Maybe whoever it was had given up.

I jumped when furious banging commenced. At this point, I was beginning to think opening the door was actually the *worst* idea. I'd left my transponder in the bedroom. Big mistake.

"Tyler!" Cassandra's voice rang through my apartment as though she had a megaphone.

My blood ran cold.

I fumbled with the locks, quickly unlatching and disengaging them.

She stood on my porch, eyes wild, hair disheveled.

"What's going on?" I asked, my voice higher than I had meant it to be.

"I've got some work for you," she said. And when my face fell in disbelief, she said, "It's urgent."

"As long as you're fairly compensating, I suppose," I said, moving deeper into my house to grab my transponder.

"Come with me," she said. "You won't be needing anything of yours; I'll provide supplies for this mission."

Something about this didn't sit right with me. Her eyes scanned my apartment, prying into my private life. One that I kept separated from work, and for good reason.

I reluctantly followed, wanting her out of my space.

Cassandra walked at breakneck speed. I wasn't sure what kind of situation I was about to find myself in, but my adrenaline was through the roof. She led me to a manhole, looking expectantly at it.

"Uh, what's down there?" I asked, not even trying to hide my skepticism.

"The rest of the group I'm assembling," replied Cassandra impatiently.

"Assembling…for what?"

"To rid our city of an infestation," growled Cassandra. "I'll brief you more when the group is all together. Now, in."

"An infestation of…what?" I asked. Were there rats in the sewers?

I looked again at the manhole cover she indicated. Yeah, *no*. I was out.

"I'm afraid you couldn't pay me enough for that." I grimaced, looking down at it.

"I'm afraid it's not optional," she quipped.

My jaw hung open. She seemed to forget that I could just walk away at any time, and just earlier this week, I had been ready to. I couldn't understand where this attitude was from.

"No, seriously," I said, crossing my arms, "I'm not touching that. Find someone else to do it."

I turned to go, done with this job and conversation. In the morning, I would pack my things and move on. There were plenty of things I could do. Maybe they weren't as cushy as this job, but this job was apparently getting less cushy by the minute.

"You're going to regret not working with me," her voice came from behind me. "You had a chance to be a hero. Oh well. I have a use for you elsewhere."

The breath rushed out of my lungs as stars filled my eyes and I fell to the ground.

My head ached. Everything was dark. I couldn't remember much, no matter how hard I tried. Cassandra's purple eyes, filled with fury, were all that came to mind. There was a roaring in my ears, and until I realized I was moving, that was all I took it to be. Hefty arms held me like a crumpled rag doll.

They set me down and I opened my eyes to see a blurry, row-dy crowd, looking at me and…someone else a few yards away. My eyes wouldn't focus enough to make out any details about him or her. I tried to raise myself up to get a better look.

Somewhere at the edge of my awareness, I heard a man's voice as if broadcast over a loudspeaker.

"…and get ready for the first fight of the night! Make some noise, Haven Club!"

CHAPTER 49

TITANIA

I was so tired. I wanted nothing more than a warm shower and maybe some more noodles. And a nap.

The date had been…wonderful. After dinner we had walked in the moonlight back to our apartment building. James escorted me to my door like a proper gentleman, and we had stood in the glow of the porch light for the longest time.

I'd nearly set the whole building on fire when he'd leaned in to kiss me. Old habits die hard! His yelp had given me plenty of time to reign it in before the fire department had to pull an all-nighter. Lucky for them, they could sleep.

Not me, though.

Sleep evaded me, even though I'd been so exhausted after I'd come inside from our date that I'd fallen right into bed without changing. I found that after dying, it was harder for me to voluntarily submit to darkness and unconsciousness. Even though it was not the same, I couldn't convince my body of that. So some nights, I stayed awake all night starting at the ceiling. Thankfully, this night I had managed to get a little bit of sleep before a nightmare woke me up. I attributed that to the high I had been on following my date with James.

Still, my mind raced. I decided that it was the uncertainty of not knowing where Silen was that was bothering me. Even though he was older and more feeble of mind now, he was still the one who did this to me. I couldn't separate the two in my mind. I couldn't convince myself that anything had significantly changed in my favor. It was crazy how I was a more powerful Titan than I ever had been, but I was still scared of a deranged old man.

Sometimes minds didn't make sense.

I climbed out of bed, anxious to walk off some of this energy. I tiptoed down the hall. I knew that Luna and James probably had enhanced hearing, too, although we'd never actually compared notes. And it wasn't like the walls were thick here…they were apartments after all.

I slipped on my shoes and a coat that would suffice, though I knew I was just going to use my powers to keep myself warm anyway.

Then, I disappeared out the door and into the night.

The air was crisp and clear. I would almost have expected snowflakes to be falling with how cold it was. Most people would've been scared of the dark, scared to walk in the abandoned streets like this. But I knew that I was by far the scariest thing on the streets right now. And this kind of darkness wasn't empty. It was just murky. There was a big, big difference between not knowing what was in the darkness and knowing that there was nothing *but* darkness.

I made my way to the gym. I couldn't say what compelled me to do it, but I felt the draw. I didn't know what I was going to do upon arriving, surely everyone was asleep. I'd figure that out when I got there, I supposed.

There were less than a handful of passersby smoking in the dark night air on the corner of the streets. They paid me no mind, and I likewise left them alone. Many of the folks here on the street were very *live and let live.* Life on the street in Reunion City was much better than life in the wilderness anywhere outside of it. The little children from the woods that I'd fed at the compound occasionally were a subject of my nightmares. I wondered what had happened to them when I left. Had they survived? I doubted the compound had. I wondered about the people who had witnessed me transform that day. I made a mental note to ask Brandon about that, when he was in a less grumpy mood from his usual. He would probably know, given all the time he spent trying to track me down. Maybe they were all told that they'd had a nervous breakdown or a mass hallucination. But I could for sure believe they had been told anything but the truth. Still, they were loose ends. I wondered if they had…*survived* witnessing me.

The gym came into sight. I walked ever closer, my hands in my pockets, until something startled me out of my leisurely walk.

A sound.

Boots echoed on the pavement of the sanctuary city behind me.

Steady. Like the sound of a heartbeat. Almost as if someone was marching. If I didn't know any better, I would say they were going to war. As I listened, I realized it was more than one person.

I looked back, transforming my eyes into that of the phoenix.

Cassandra.

The DNA had helped to amplify the sound in my ears from a ways off, even when I wasn't actively relying on it. It wasn't just her marching toward our part of town. There was a host of people with her. I couldn't imagine what would've warranted such a lovely visit, but I didn't have a good feeling about it. It was never a good thing to be visited by Cassandra, in my opinion, but I definitely didn't want to be visited by Cassandra and all of her closest friends…if we could call them that. I wasn't even sure that she had real friends.

I wished that I could spread my wings and land on the roof to get a better view, but that would be conspicuous.

I decided to hightail it to the gym and try to raise the alarm with the others. I wasn't sure what we should prepare for, but I was certain it was something. I wondered if Cassandra could see me under the cover of darkness. I didn't want to go off in a sprint and make her even more suspicious. But I wanted to warn the others before she got there. I could already see Adam's displeased face about me waking him up before the crack of dawn. Whatever. He'd thank me later.

Cassandra couldn't possibly have heard me leaving my apartment and followed me, could she? I didn't actually know where she called home in Reunion City, although I had always assumed it was her office.

Suddenly, a tall figure appeared beside me, slipping out of a dark alleyway. I nearly jumped into the air before James' face materialized out of the murkiness of the night. I looked back to see if Cassandra was still following, but if she was, she was too far back for me to see.

"What are you doing here?" I asked, eyeing James up and down as he smirked so salaciously that it made me want to smack him.

"I couldn't sleep," he said with a shrug, as though it was the most normal thing in the world to follow a girl around in the middle of the night. I noticed that his sleeve was longer than his arm. Was he still wearing his suit from our date?

I stepped closer.

Yep. He was.

Boys were so silly.

"That doesn't seem like the most comfortable thing to sleep in, you know? Maybe that's why you couldn't sleep," I said quietly.

"You're one to talk," he teased, gesturing at my dress before frowning. "Why are you whispering?"

I took his hand and started walking. I didn't want Cassandra to catch up to us before we could get to the others. Between coming out unscathed in the aftermath of fire, my personal interrogation with Cassandra, Greg's own run-in with her, and then sneaking in and out of the fighting ring, I was just sure that our luck with her was running out somehow.

"I'll tell you in a little bit. Where's Brandon?"

"He's at home, asleep. Why?"

I was contemplating what would happen with Brandon if something happened to us. We had no way to contact him, that I knew of, to let him know that something was wrong. If she was coming to do more than pay a little visit, we could all be wiped out without anyone saying a word or finding us.

I liked our odds, but I didn't like putting the kids in a frontline situation. They were just kids. They didn't need to be in danger like this. It wasn't like we could call the police. If the mayor of the city had it out for us, it wasn't like they would be on our side.

"I think Cassandra is coming. I saw and heard her behind me. I was just out for a walk because I couldn't sleep either."

"More nightmares?" James interjected.

"Yeah," I said. "Anyway, she didn't seem to be alone, and she was walking this way."

I cast a nervous glance behind me.

"Are you sure you weren't just seeing things from being overly tired?" James asked. I supposed he would know, given that he had been a medic, that that could happen. But I still didn't like the implication that I might be a little crazy.

His search for anyone behind us in the darkness came up empty, and I could see why he would conclude that. But I knew what I saw. She was out there.

"Come on," I said, picking up the pace as I held his hand. As long as we could get to the gym before something happened, I could warn the others and we could come up with a plan.

CHAPTER 50

MELODY

Toys went skittering across the floor as I dropped them. A knock at the door? It had to be past midnight!

I wheeled to the door to answer it.

"Hello?" I said, peeking out.

A frazzled James and Titania stood in the dark of the night.

"Come in!" I wheeled backward, making room for them to follow.

James quickly locked the door behind them.

"What's going on?"

"I think something is about to happen." Titania's face was ashen. "Cassandra is coming, and she seems to be bringing friends."

"Why would she be coming here?" I asked, frowning. I'd just gotten all the kids to bed. They were *supposed* to be asleep, anyway…

When they all came pouring out of the hallway, it didn't come as a shock, though.

"Maybe she clocked Adam in the tunnels?" James offered.

Titania nodded. "That would make sense. I don't know how she's going to feel about us knowing about that secret arena."

Luna had filled me in on a little of it. From the sound of it, I was surprised Cassandra hadn't thrown some of the kids into the fighting ring. It seems to be half circus, half fight club. They were the perfect specimens for it.

My eyes went wide. What if she was coming for them now?

"One second." I held up a finger to James and Titania, turning around to face my little army.

I whistled, getting the attention of all the kids. Dozens of little eyes peered up at me.

"I have a big job, are you ready for it?"

They all excitedly exclaimed, "Yes!"

"I need everyone to help me check locks on all the windows and doors to the outside. I'll give each of you two extra rides in the morning. Ready? Go!"

"Genius," James mumbled.

I smiled.

"I'll go let Jen and Adam know," I said. "You stay here and watch that door."

Adam met me in the hall, already halfway awake, so I quickly relayed the news. "Something's up. Cassandra is on her way, and it doesn't seem to be a friendly visit."

I wheeled past him, going to knock on Jen's door. She peeked up, more peeved than I had ever seen her before. I always saw her so put together, but her bed head looked like a bird had nested in it. "We've got a situation." I grimaced.

She nodded wordlessly, pulling her door closed behind her.

I made it back into the gym in time for all of the kids to pour out of the crevices in the building and report back.

"Melody, Melody!" The little skunk boy burst into the room. "We dinnent see any unlocked winnowth or doorths. Can I have a thnack now?"

CHAPTER 51

NATALIE

Vaulting over the window as a mouse was a bit trickier than as a cat like Miranda. Still, I wasn't super happy to have gotten the lift Miranda gave me. Her teeth sunk into my neck and adrenaline flowed through me as my body and DNA feared the worst. She was a predator, and I was the prey.

She jumped with me in tow, and just like that, we were on the outside. She carried me around, prancing on her little fluffy paws despite my protestations for her to put me down. I could run on my own little legs.

We rounded the corner to find a whole cast of characters waiting at the front door of the gymnasium. Some looked like normal human beings, but others looked as though they might be Titans, too. That did not sit well with me. The ramifications of that were more than I could think through in the moment.

There was Cassandra, a few other folks that haunted her office that I recognized, and many that I did not. I couldn't imagine what they were all doing here. And unlike her, some of them seemed like a motley crew. They weren't all prim and polished.

In fact, some of them looked like they had been swimming in the sewer.

We sized them up, my dignity dying every second that Miranda held me in her mouth.

"We'll be in soon enough," we heard Cassandra mutter under her breath. Animal hearing was good for picking up things that people didn't actually want you to hear.

Miranda backed up, trying to stay out of sight and suspicion. But Cassandra's purple eyes tracked the movement immediately. She opened her mouth, then sneered. Her fist balled up as she started stalking toward us.

Her eyes had always creeped me out. I had to assume they were contacts.

Miranda put it into high gear, speeding around the corner and back to our window. I bounced helplessly, hopelessly, as we drifted around and toward our entry point. The only problem was, if Cassandra saw us go in that way, could she come through the window? I thought she was too big, but I wasn't sure that other participants in her party wouldn't be the right fit. And even if she didn't fit, she could always bust out the window and send a drone in or something. Maybe I was overthinking it. Maybe Miranda had shaken me a little bit too much, like what people always said about babies. Can't shake them, it'll rattle their brains.

Just as I was contemplating if I could be salvaged, Miranda made an ambitious leap up and over the window.

We skidded to a halt on top of a table. Miranda's paws were immediately transforming into hands as she started the process of going back to human. The windowpane proved to be difficult to close halfway in and out of human and cat, but she managed it just in the nick of time, crushing Cassandra's grimy fingers.

She cried out in pain, an alarmingly shrill sound piercing the tiny room.

Seconds later, the door burst open as Titania came to investigate what was going on. Her eyes went wide as she shooed Miranda and me out of the room. I saw the flame rising up in her hands as she approached the window. If there was one person I really wouldn't want to be in that moment, it was Cassandra.

I had no problem evacuating the area. Our mission was complete. My legs found purchase under me as I transformed into a human again, and I went in search of Adam to report our findings.

He was not pensive when we located him in the corner of the gym, but he was militantly focused on what needed to happen.

Adam soaked up every bit of information with clear eyes and confidence.

CHAPTER 52

TITANIA

Cassandra pulled against the window crushing her fingers. She tugged furiously as one of her cronies came around from the side of the building to assist her, her screams beckoning for help.

I had little sympathy for her, but I wasn't going to hurt her unless she hit first. The flames in my hands were nothing more than an intimidation tactic. And by the look on her face, I would wager it was working.

I drew closer, inching forward menacingly. I knew how she liked to play games, and I was willing to speak her language for a second if it meant she called off the dogs.

Her fingers finally popped out from under the window, and I closed it as she looked at them in horror and howled. I had no doubt it hurt. But she was the one ambushing us in the middle of the night, so I couldn't be too sympathetic.

Her purple eyes flashed at me in the dark night, highlighted only by the moon.

But she didn't approach the window. She backed away and followed the man who had come to help her, walking around to the other side of the building. I was a little bit hesitant to abandon this window now that they knew about it being a viable entrance. I extinguished the flames and made sure to lock it all up again.

Then I rushed out to the gymnasium area, catching Natalie, Miranda, and Adam in a huddle in the hallway.

"There are a lot of people out there," Natalie said worriedly. It was in her nature to be worried. I sometimes wondered if it was because she was such a small creature, her animal mind making her a little more susceptible to being scared of things. Whereas, with Miranda being a predator, she was more brash and sure of herself. She had markedly fewer fears…especially when one considered that she was allergic to her own foreign DNA. I would never get used to seeing a human face with whiskers on it, but that was what she had to do to keep her reactions at bay.

"We'll get it taken care of," Adam assured them both.

He shot me a look that didn't exactly convey the same sentiment. If I had to translate it, I would've said it delivered an idea of just how much of a fight we had ahead of us.

From the sound of things, we didn't have very long before they bust open that front door. I wished that we could've gotten everyone evacuated, but we didn't have any good options for that. And besides, I thought that everyone was tired of running. I knew that I was. We needed some place where we didn't have to run anymore. This was supposed to be that place.

"How about you stand guard with the kids?" I offered to the both of them.

Miranda shook her head. "If there is a fight, I'm in. I have some unresolved anger issues that would be perfectly resolved with a satisfying smack to these people's faces."

That was infinitely fair and understandable.

Natalie agreed to my suggestion, though. She skittered off to stand guard in front of the kids.

"Let's go," I said to Adam and Miranda. We marched onward.

I stopped in my tracks as I took in Jen…as an elephant. She was far larger than I anticipated. And to be completely honest, she looked angry. Really, *really* angry.

Despite the younger kids being put away in a safe space, we still had quite a crew. As long as Cassandra wasn't fighting dirty, we should be fine…

The door started giving way. James was near the front, his eyebrows knit together. He looked back at me, nodding.

Take care of yourself was the wordless message.

He would be so upset if I got hurt. He still didn't understand that I might be the scariest thing in this gym.

Adam fanned out to go be next to Luna, who was already down on all fours, snarling like she was about to personally give every single one of these intruders rabies. I couldn't blame her.

Miranda went to a bored-looking Trevor, who was waiting flanking the left side of the door.

I couldn't imagine how these people thought they were going to get through us. Or why.

The door swung open, finally giving way. Jen stood above all of us, and in a frenzy, people started pouring in. She tried to stop them, which sent us all flying in different directions either from the impact or to avoid being squashed. We hadn't really thought this through. I focused, growing out my wings. They ripped through my dress. I supposed that I couldn't have nice things forever, but I was sad it only lasted one night.

I felt like I was seconds away from becoming a squashed grape.

Melody wheeled around in her chair, trying to be in a safe place. I wasn't really sure what she was going to do, but when I heard an agonizing scream come from a man, I looked over to find she was running over people's toes in her wheelchair. I was impressed, despite my grimacing. I had nearly been a victim of that recently and I did not envy them. It was a brilliant strategy. They'd never assume she could really do much to them, and then she'd brutally murder all of their toes.

A man charged at me at full speed and I erupted into flames. That usually gave people a moment's pause, but he didn't even hesitate. I did not like that. Usually, people were a little bit more concerned about barreling toward a person on fire.

He brought a fisted hand down, trying to bludgeon me with his arm. I stopped it, but as I held his arm in my hand, I realized that his sleeve was burning away without him screaming or crying out in pain. Knocked off-kilter by that, he was able to shove me back while revealing a metal arm. It was only just beginning to start surrendering to the fire.

A cyborg?

How could this man be a cyborg?

His face looked somewhat familiar. I racked my brain trying to come up with where I could have possibly seen him. Around the city, maybe? Cassandra's purple eyes flashed from the doorway behind him as she surveyed the deluge of fighting in front of her. Per usual, she was happy to stand back and let other people get their hands dirty.

The cyborg man charged me again, and this time, I took off into the air. I'd much rather expend the energy keeping myself afloat than I would fighting someone taller than me *and* with metal arms. At least this way I could just kick him in the face.

Though I did wonder something. My wings held me aloft and out of reach, which elicited an aggravated look from him. I held my hands out in front of me, forming the fire balls I had been practicing as of late. I had been wanting to try something out, but I hadn't had a good place to do it. I felt like it would be conspicuous if I threw fire balls at a random empty building out here. If someone did happen upon the charred remnants of something like that, there would be a lot of explaining to do.

But…

I wanted to know something.

I held myself just above the man as he grasped for my feet, jumping to try and pull me back down. I had to stay far enough above him that he couldn't get to me. I faltered as I tried to focus on both creating the fire balls and staying aloft.

I managed to do it, it just took a lot of concentration. My head ached from it. I drew back my arm, as though I was about to throw a ball.

The man didn't so much as flinch. Was I just kidding myself? This probably wouldn't work, and then I would look stupid.

I willed the fire to leave my grasp. I tried to coax it to go beyond my fingertips and stay cohesive enough to hit him. And while it did travel farther than I expected to, it did little more than singe his eyebrows.

Kicking toward the man's head, my foot found purchase and scuffed up his face. I quickly launched myself higher into the air. Behind the man, one of the kids—a girl with a tentacle arm—

was slowly positioning herself. I tried to keep my face blank. I wasn't sure what she was planning, but I definitely did not want to give away her location.

He didn't seem to notice. The murderous glare told me everything I needed to know about how he felt at this point. I zigged and zagged just above him, trying to keep him distracted.

The girl wrapped her tentacle around his waist, holding him in place. I took my opportunity to get in a few good kicks, until his nose began to bleed. We just needed to run these people off. As long as they knew we were stronger, they'd leave us alone. Except for maybe Cassandra. She would have to be dealt with, but the rest of these cronies were just her henchmen. I doubted they cared about us beyond just doing what she told them to.

"Thanks," I said to the girl with the tentacle arm as the man held up his hands in front of himself, desperate for the wailing to stop. She beamed at me proudly. I yanked the man's arm, interested in seeing what kind of metal it was that had withstood the heat I produced. I couldn't tell much.

The man oscillated between looking like he was going to cower and looking like he was going to pick back up with our little squabble.

The noise within the gymnasium was at a deafening level. There were people crying out in pain, battle cries that reverberated throughout the building, and random animal noises. Everything around here was always punctuated by random animal noises, so much so that, most of the time, my brain filtered them out. I saw Trevor bite down particularly hard on someone's leg in my peripheral vision and winced. My hostage took advantage of the distraction and put me in a headlock with his metal arm. He was surprisingly quick and agile.

I squirmed, confident in my ability to get away from him. But my confidence started bleeding out at a frantic pace as my attempts weren't producing the results I had hoped for. I couldn't bite him—his arm wasn't made of flesh. I set my whole body ablaze, knowing that, while his arm was metal, some part of him had to be real. *That* got a response.

He set me loose like a hot potato, shoving me away from him.

I didn't want to look at him. I hadn't really wanted to do that. If he would've just played nice, I wouldn't have had to. But I already knew the outcome…he was burned. I just didn't know how badly. I didn't want to know.

"If you had any sense, you'd face me. It's dishonorable to not face your opponent, even if you've won."

I turned around, caught between wanting to defend myself and not wanting to see his face.

I was aghast to find that part of his face, now completely exposed beneath the flesh on his cheek, was also metal. It was one thing to have foreign DNA flowing through your veins—I could still look human, most of us could. And I supposed this man could, too, but I had to imagine it was so much more difficult to lie to yourself that nothing had changed when you looked like that.

I shuddered.

"You're weak," he said. "You're allowing the humanity you have to overshadow your potential."

CHAPTER 53

URBAN EXPLORERS

"Are you sure about this?" the redheaded boy asked his friend, nervously glancing up as his companion went up dilapidated stairs. "You remember what happened last time," he reminded him, not wanting a repeat. There might not be someone around this time to help them, and if there was, they might not be as merciful as last time. If their parents found out they were urban exploring, let alone after dark, they'd be grounded for life. Forget *urban* exploration, they wouldn't even be able to explore their own backyard. Well, if they had a backyard to explore.

"It'll be fine." The sandy-haired boy waved him off, brushing aside his concerns.

He made it to the top, triumphant.

"See!" he said, bragging. "I told you it would be fine.

Then the floor shifted beneath them, sending the sandy-haired boy at the top of the stairs grappling for something to hang on to. His friend at the bottom gasped, nervous energy exuding from him.

"What was that?" he whimpered.

The sandy-haired boy sat down, descending the stairs one by one on his backside.

"I don't know." His voice was filled with trepidation, less assured than he had been before.

"Maybe an earthquake?" the redheaded boy offered.

"That didn't sound like any earthquake I've ever heard." The sandy-haired boy shook his head in disagreement.

His friend at the bottom of the stairs shifted nervously.

"What could it be?" he asked.

Then the building shook again, and he found his hands were getting cold from adrenaline.

"I don't know," the sandy-haired boy said as he reached the bottom, "but I'm going to find out."

The redheaded boy trembled as he followed his companion through the dark and out the door into the night.

CHAPTER 54

BRANDON

Brandon had awoken to James being gone. Which wouldn't have been unusual, except he'd heard James come in for the night from his date. He was humming a song that rang a bell in the recesses of Brandon's mind. It must've gone well, he thought, before he drifted back to sleep. But he'd awoken with a start, unsure of what had caused it. The apartment was quiet, without a single sound but the humming of the refrigerator.

When he'd gone to look for James, his intuition screaming at him, he'd turned up empty in his search. Had he been kidnapped? Brandon was not up for another rescue mission so soon.

But then he felt it, more so in his bionic arm than anywhere else. It didn't diffuse movement in the same way that his human flesh did. He strained, trying to hear anything that accompanied the movement. Falling short, he grabbed his coat and descended the stairs. He was far faster on his own two feet than he was taking the elevator.

Blood rushed in his ears as the night air caught him by surprise with its sharpness. He missed the warmth of the desert he had spent so much time in over the past few years.

As he walked, he realized that he was going in the wrong direction. The vibrations were becoming more and more faint. He wondered if there was some kind of ballistics testing going on in the area. It seemed unlikely, but anything was possible.

Once he was sure he was moving in the correct direction, he picked up the pace. He did not like that James was missing and that there were explosive shocks hitting the ground here. His friend seemed to be a magnet for trouble, and as he thought back, he supposed that had always been true. The amount of things that had been confiscated from the two of them over the years, the adventures they had. Maybe they were *both* magnets for trouble, and that's perhaps how Brandon found himself in this situation in the first place.

The trek to discover the origin of this mysterious phenomenon was made shorter by the fact that he did not like this cold and did not want to stay in it any longer than he had to. There had been a reason that he had henchmen working for him. He liked sending younger, more able-bodied people out in the cold. Extreme weather made his metal arm ache, if that was even a thing. Perhaps they were just phantom pains. But they were unpleasant, and they made him recall things that he didn't ever want to think about again.

The sooner he found James, the better.

Two figures came into view, only barely illuminated at their edges by the light pouring out of an open door. It bathed what little part of the night it touched with illumination. Squinting, Brandon realized that neither of the two were the correct height or frame to be James. He grimaced. Who were they? Judging by their size, they were far too young to be wandering the streets of a city at night. Where was their mother? Probably sound asleep in her bed without a clue that they were running the streets. Zero sense of self-preservation, Brandon thought.

Just then, a woman practically flew out of the doorway, skidding across the asphalt with impressive force. When she found her bearings, Brandon's stomach twisted like a knife had been driven straight through him. He wasn't sure if he knew the woman personally, but he had not a doubt in his mind that he knew *of* her.

Most bionics did. Whether it was by choice, by force, or by urban legend, he didn't know a single person who was unaware of this woman's existence.

The woman with purple eyes had a lot to answer for.

As she lunged at the children, one cowering in fear and one running for his life, he knew that he couldn't let her lay a finger on them.

He threw himself in her path, more than ready for the fight that was to come.

CHAPTER 55

URBAN EXPLORERS

The sound and the shaking were only getting more prominent. With each passing moment, the boys struggled to remain upright on the road.

The redheaded boy voiced a concern. "What if we should be running away from this?"

His sandy-haired companion dismissed him outright. "No, something is happening and I want to know what."

The redheaded boy reluctantly followed, reaching out to brace himself against the world, which seemed to tip from side to side as they went.

If he hadn't already lived through some earthquakes, he would've assumed this was one. It didn't have the right feel though; this was something different.

They neared a building they had once explored, or at least tried to. The one where the ladies had found them and rescued them. They both slowed down, remembering the warning they had been given that day.

But curiosity overtook them.

They pushed forward. Up ahead, light poured out of a door.

They shared a look, moving to conceal themselves in shadows. The noise was now overwhelmingly loud, and while the shaking had calmed down some, every few seconds it started back up again.

Did they dare look? As they crept toward the door, a woman flew backward through it. Her purple eyes shot daggers at them as they came into her field of vision. The boys froze instinctually, hoping that she wouldn't turn that energy on them. She sneered, rising to her feet and moving toward them. The sandy-haired boy found his footing, beginning to run away. But the redheaded boy stood like a statue, anchored to the cold street.

He shrieked as the woman lunged toward him, but something peculiar happened.

A man leapt in front of her, cutting off her assault.

Relief filled both boys, mixed with uncertainty and adrenaline.

"You need to get out of here," the man growled.

The gulp that the redheaded boy swallowed was visible as it bobbed down his throat. Before he could turn to run, their savior clashed with the purple-eyed woman, and another person rushed out from the door.

It was the girl in the wheelchair. She looked more disheveled than she had before, but her determination was evident on her face. She recognized them immediately, and they knew that—if they survived this—there would inevitably be a lecture. They just didn't know who from or how many lectures they might receive.

She rushed toward them, drawing them away from the action.

"What's happening?" the sandy-haired boy asked her, his voice cracking with fear.

"It's complicated," the girl said, her eyes sympathetic but full of disappointment. "But you guys really shouldn't be seeing this."

It bothered the sandy-haired boy that she was talking down to them. She couldn't have been any older than he was, and here she was acting like she could be part of the action and they couldn't. She was even a girl! What did girls know about fighting?

Behind her, the man that had intervened to save them used his right hand to stop a punch that the woman with purple eyes leveled at him.

The boys watched with anxious anticipation as they went 'round and 'round. The man and woman seemed to be talking, but neither boy could make out what they were saying over the deluge of other yells and sounds pouring out of the front door.

The wheelchair girl nearly ran them over as she herded them further away, the lone battle encroaching on their space a short distance away.

The man sent a punch straight into the woman's abdomen, and for a moment, they saw her falter. Something about that seemed personal, the sandy-haired boy thought. Did they know each other?

CHAPTER 56

ADAM

I sighed.

This was going to be a headache to deal with later.

I dodged a punch thrown at my head. No need to anticipate two headaches.

Jen really needed a miniature elephant setting. While she had maimed quite a few of our enemies, we'd had some near misses. For as collected and focused as she was as a human, she was very much *not* as an elephant. While proving to be a very helpful way to disorient the enemy, there were downsides.

I wondered if she was getting tired of stomping around and honking. She seemed to be slowing down.

When I'd seen some of these people underneath the city, I never actually thought we'd be fighting any of them. And now that we were, I was even more upset for that little girl that they'd stuck in the ring. How she was still alive, I couldn't fathom. She was notably absent from the fray here, and I wondered where she was.

Once I sent Cassandra flying out the door, after she dogpiled me while I was dealing with one of her cronies, I decided that we were going to have to figure out a different living situation…in record time. There was no way we could stay here.

I ducked, barely missing a punch to the side of my face. The man growled as he tried to catch himself. I noticed he wasn't great with his balance. He may have superstrength or some kind of enhancement, but he seemed a little slow and unsure of himself. I considered shifting, but it honestly seemed like that was what they were wanting from us. As soon as we transformed, the pressure went from zero to sixty. They directed far more energy and attention to those of us who were shifted than they did to those of us who still looked human.

It left me uneasy. And because Titania had transformed, they of course were spending a lot of resources on her. She was flying circles over them—for the most part—but if I didn't know any better, I would say she was getting a little cocky. I didn't like it.

The logistics of this battle were an absolute nightmare. While we'd taken out quite a few of our assailants, there were still some heavy hitters in the fray. Trevor took it upon himself to drag the unconscious ones to the wall, lining them up in their shame. What were we going to do with them when they woke up? This was not exactly laying low. All of these people were witnesses to what we could do. What we were. It was ironic that, despite Cassandra saying that she wanted us to stay under the radar, she'd now led a bunch of people straight to us. She must've assumed she was going to win.

Miranda bit down on one of the rugged-looking women hard. I winced in sympathy as she drew back, the woman grabbing her new puncture wound. Even though Miranda was human, all of us could give people the infections that were present in our animal form. That lady was going to have to be treated with antibiotics most likely, and I'd have to probably figure out how to do that myself, because otherwise that was going to be quite the story she told to the ER. Although…if we could spin it as a bunch of people who had a strange infection or had maybe consumed one of the iridescent, glowing mushrooms or other plants in the woods, we could maybe discredit their entire witness against us. It wasn't like there hadn't been mass hallucinations in history before. It was believable.

I was intentionally having to avoid listening in on animal minds in the gym because, otherwise, my eyes would've crossed. Besides, it was trivially easy to detect these fighters next steps. They telegraphed them just as much in these fights as they did in the underground ring.

There was one voice that I wished I could hear—that of the little girl's—but it was nowhere to be found.

CHAPTER 57

MELODY

The sound of metal scraping metal rang out into the night. The fighters performed their little song and dance, airing out their grievances without a word uttered to each other, for an audience of me and two curious boys. I could hear the oohs and aahs as though we were simply watching a movie.

The woman with the purple eyes was Cassandra. I knew that from having heard Jen's description of her in the short time I'd been here. That young man, though, I wasn't familiar with. His right sleeve fluttered whenever he threw a punch and I saw a metallic glint underneath. Whenever Cassandra blocked one of his blows, it made a sound like a hammer striking an anvil. Just what were these two?

In one of the most insane turn of events, Titania's harried next-door neighbor snagged Cassandra as she tried to evade the metal man. Still reeling from the last blow she'd dealt to him, he wasn't on his A game.

But Greg, ever the fashionable oddity, stood in the cold with his house slippers and tan trench coat, wrapped around Cassandra like he was making a citizen's arrest.

"That was quite the show," he guffawed.

I wheeled over to him, wondering how long he had been watching. The two boys who were definitely *not* supposed to be here looked increasingly worried. They'd added another witness to the list of people who could tell their mamas that they were out on the streets of the city in the middle of the night.

I wondered what Greg had picked up on. He already thought that I was just cosplaying, but I wasn't sure if he'd noticed the metal that the young man was sporting. To be completely honest, I had questions about that situation myself.

Every day since I became a lab-made monstrosity was a day where the questions mounted. At least now, I could ask them.

The metal man recovered enough to step up to the plate next to Greg and march Cassandra in between the two of them. There was a lot less shaking of the ground, and as I crossed the threshold to the gym behind them, I didn't see any sign of Jen. It was kind of difficult to misplace an elephant.

The inside of the gym looked like nobody had won this battle. There were bodies propped up along the wall, though when I looked closely, all of them were still breathing. They were pretty banged up, though. I wondered if Adam and James were going to have to patch them all up themselves.

What were we going to do with all of these people? What were we going to do with Cassandra?

A million questions flew through my head.

Adam, James, and Titania were all on their feet. Everyone else could barely claim the same, or were resting on their knees with heaving breaths. Those who couldn't remain upright were all lying down on the floor wherever they'd been at the end of the fight. Trevor looked like he'd run several marathons consecutively, but it seemed that Miranda's presence right next to him eased the burden. His grin was massive. I sometimes felt like his skin had a lizard-like quality, even when he wasn't transformed.

Natalie was frowning looking over the mess of the gym.

From the back room, the children talked a million miles an hour. It was hard to discern what they were saying. Before I went off to go check on them, Brandon threw Cassandra into a circle with Adam, James, and Titania.

"What are we going to do with her?"

Greg stood, his arms crossed, blending in as though he were one of the team.

She glowered at them all, a bit of blood mixing with her saliva as it dripped down her teeth. I was quite surprised that she hadn't had any of them knocked out in the fight.

They were all silent. Perhaps they were too tired or just thinking. The children sounded like they were going to bust down the door at any moment.

"I imagine that the government would love to be aware of all of the laws you've been breaking," Brandon said with a smirk.

"What laws?" she spat back at him. "This is a sanctuary city. I say what goes on here and what doesn't."

"That's true," Brandon said, rubbing his hand over his chin, "but other countries have laws about what happens to things imported here, and I do believe you've broken quite a few of them…"

Her face paled, making her purple eyes pop all the more.

"What are you talking about?"

"Oh, a little birdie told me all about how some of your little friends here landed in the US. *And* the conditions upon which they were sold."

"A snitch?" she shrieked, lunging.

Titania and James held her back, saddling her with a disapproving glance.

"Let's just say, you ought to be more careful about who you consider friends." Brandon winked.

He put all of his weight on one foot and crossed his arms.

"Shall we send you to trial for your crimes, or should we just let you loose in the wilderness and make sure you never get the chance to harm another person again?"

She gulped, then struggled with all of her might. She wrestled one of her arms out of Titania's grasp, but Adam quickly got her back in check, rather roughly.

"Let's sleep on it." James flashed him a look. "Tonight we can keep her in the cell we kept Silen in. He didn't get out by himself; she should be safe there."

"And what about the rest of them?"

"I'll take care of that," Adam volunteered.

James looked a little surprised but nodded.

"It's settled, then. We'll figure the rest out in the morning."

With that out of the way, I wheeled down the hall to some very hyper, overly sleep-deprived children. I took a deep breath before turning the knob and opening the floodgates.

CHAPTER 58

CAELUS

The eye whirred as the subject came into focus. While their operative might not be helpful beyond this point, they had certainly gleaned a wealth of knowledge and information out of the individual. And even when the camera inside of the bionic cornea became damaged from the punches, they were still able to harvest biometric data on the subjects in question.

The government, for however powerful they might be in comparison to their enemies, didn't have endless resources. They could posture that they did all day long, send out such posturing over radio and television, to whatever municipalities still had such luxuries. But in reality, their best intel was gathered by people who weren't particularly expensive to employ, and not particularly skilled either. And in this case, the individual was completely oblivious. The subject had no idea that the eye was a camera. They were unlikely to ever find out, and even if they did, there was nothing that they could do about it, anyway.

The person reviewing the footage winced with every blow, taking the damage sustained personally.

"That's a shame.," came whispered beneath their breath, "That was such a nice camera."

The wall contained rows and rows of monitors, some with still frames of the subjects, and others with videos. There was no doubt that the subjects were persons of particular interest. The question remained, were these the *only* subjects remaining? Recordkeeping had become particularly dicey as vigilantes had broken in at various locations, disgruntled employees had absconded with information, and certain experiments had vanished without a trace. But this was still a solvable, manageable situation that didn't rise to the level of a crisis. Not yet, anyway.

CHAPTER 59

TITANIA

"I thought we were safe here," I said to the group of us walking back to the apartment. Somehow, I felt that this was all my fault. If I was really as strong as Silen said I was, I should've been able to stop all of this immediately.

It was an apology as much as it was anything else. I looked up to find Brandon staring directly at me. From the look on his face, I couldn't tell if he was angry with me or pitying me. Either way, I fidgeted uncomfortably.

After a silence that stretched for half a block, he spoke. "Safety is an illusion, Titania. The sooner you learn that, the sooner you'll be free from the pretense of not having to sleep with one eye open."

I bit my lip. That was not comforting. I was so stupid. We should've never considered ourselves safe here. I had been delusional to ever believe it.

"It's time to stop and rest," Greg said, his hands firmly planted on my arms. He waved at the others to keep going.

He must've seen right through me. Through the war I was fighting in between my ears.

While the others were more or less confident in Adam and James' abilities to figure this out, I was not. I wanted to pace until I burned a crevice into the street, while waiting for my wings to carry me away without me even having to think about it.

It was odd to be touched without hesitation. I had to remind myself that Greg had not been around for my sizzling skin on contact era.

His eyes searched me, trying to grab onto the anxiety that was swirling through me.

If we weren't safe here, we weren't safe anywhere. We'd lived in a cave, an abandoned building, in plain sight, and now in this city. And eventually, trouble always found us. Or we found it. I wasn't sure which. How could we possibly keep doing this? We had no safe place to land!

"Titania," he said, trying to get me to make eye contact, "I know you're scared. But we're not going to let anything happen to you guys here."

He looked toward the two teenage boys shivering near the wall ahead of us. We really needed to take them home.

I wasn't sure how much they could secure a safe place for us, but I supposed I appreciated the sentiment.

"I'm serious," he insisted. "We're not going to let anything happen."

Was this what having a father was like? An older man standing up for you? I was caught off guard by emotion. I knew he wasn't lying, I just didn't know where his abilities ended and his optimism began.

"There are plenty of people that have lived in peace with you guys for months, well, a year really, for everyone else. You've made connections. You all have friends."

That was such a foreign concept to me. In the compound, you didn't necessarily have friends. You had people that you saw every day, people that you worked with, people everywhere. But that didn't mean that you had an ally in anyone. We always had to watch our back. Whether it was an accident, or minor infraction, or a little teenage rebellion…someone was always ready to snitch.

We had to watch our backs. And here Greg was, offering to watch our backs for us.

"Thanks," I said, realizing that the adrenaline was waning and I was actually really, *really* tired. Maybe I did just need some sleep before I made any hasty decisions.

"Let's get everyone home," Greg said, taking me under his arm.

He was right. The night was over.

For tonight, we had a safe haven.

The morning would be a mystery.

CHAPTER 60

THE LITTLE GIRL

Everything was a blur of motion and sound, footsteps, and frantic talking. Sleep clung to the little girl like a heavy fog. She hardly had time to wonder where it was she was going. They hadn't even expected her to walk this time. She was cradled in the arms of one of the large men that had been part of the regular round of faces she saw. He could've easily been mistaken for just another performer in the little circus that ran beneath the city. Her eyes opened enough for her to recognize they were going underneath the arch that led into the arena. She wondered if she would have to climb those dreadful stairs again. There was no way, she thought, that he could safely carry her up them. But to her surprise, he turned in the opposite direction.

No sooner had they crossed over the bridge than he turned on his heel and marched her in the direction of the dark tunnel to the left. She wondered what could be this way. She'd never been this way before, and she hadn't ever seen anyone else travel in this direction, either. Her body involuntarily shivered as they passed beyond where the light from the arena reached. They'd been plunged into total darkness.

Her eyes adjusted quickly, but there wasn't much for her to see. Just a seemingly endless expanse of more tunnel, with occasional breaks in one direction or another. The little girl was beginning to think that they would walk in a straight line forever, never seeing the daylight again. It occurred to her that the man might not even know where he was going, and that they would find themselves lost.

But then he turned, going right, which also appeared to be little more than an endless expanse of tunnel ahead of them.

She contemplated going back to sleep. But the fear of him slipping and dropping her kept her from dozing off again. She'd rather be prepared to land on her feet than risk falling and hitting her head or tumbling into the sewage.

Antsy and agitated, she began to squirm.

"Stay put," the man told her, a little gruffly. She frowned, feeling more confined by the minute. She was, of course, used to a certain threshold for the feeling, but this was quickly becoming intolerable.

Then, she noticed something.

They were not alone.

At least, she didn't think they were. Her head perked up, scanning inside of the darkness for signs of another person, or thing. She sniffed, getting the faintest smell of something other than the waste below them and the scent of her captor.

This was something else. Something new. Some*one* new.

She called out in the darkness, despite knowing that nobody could hear her. And even when she didn't get a response, she didn't lose hope. There was definitely something, or someone, down there besides them.

CHAPTER 61

MELODY

The children were finally settled down, with their murmurs and whispers fading into nothing as they all fell asleep. Adam was tending to the injured, keeping them locked away in another part of the gym. Titania had gone with Brandon to walk the two boys home. And Jen was unconscious, lying on a couch. I was nervous when I had seen her in that state, but Adam seemed completely unbothered by it. So did Luna. I wondered if this was why Jen didn't really transform frequently. I couldn't blame her. Luna sat next to her, just monitoring occasionally, and the rest of the time, staring into oblivion. Natalie and Miranda dozed off beside her on the couch. They looked like a bunch of cats in a cuddle puddle, especially with Miranda's whiskers being so prominent on her face.

We were all tired. None of us could've prepared for an onslaught after dark like that.

A noise startled me. I couldn't be sure if I had even heard anything. Luna didn't move from where she was, and the others still slept soundly.

I replayed it in my mind, trying to figure out what it had been. I tried to let it go, especially since I hadn't heard anything else in the intervening time. But it bothered me. Especially after the evening we had.

"Did you hear that?" I inquired in Luna's general direction. But she was not responsive. I decided to just put my fears to rest. I was just hearing things from being overly tired.

I grabbed the wheels of my chair and pushed, propelling myself to the door. I made swift work of the lock and pulled it open, looking out into the open street. There was nothing. No sudden movement, no sound, no shadowy figures. I started to reverse but stopped dead in my tracks.

At my feet lay a boy who looked close to my age. And he was out cold. I suppressed a scream. I did not want to get the kids all riled up again. Part of me wondered if this was some kind of trap. Could he be faking it? I watched as his back rose and fell from his breathing. I poked my fin at him, at a loss for what else to do. But he didn't move.

I sighed, bracing myself. I didn't recognize him from the fight. I racked my brain. I let the door close gently before wheeling over to Luna.

"Hey," I said, feeling awful for pulling her out of her trance.

"Huh?" she said with startled panic. "What?"

"There's someone at the door," I whispered, trying not to wake the sleeping girls or children. "Will you come look?"

"What?" she rasped, rubbing her temples.

She rose, her gray and blonde hair falling down behind her back. I followed behind her as she made short work of the distance and opened the door. I half expected him to be gone. I was still trying to convince myself I hadn't hallucinated him when she hoisted him up in her arms. I held the door open as she marched his body inside, his head flopping around as she carried him.

She headed in Adam's direction. I stayed in the gym. Whatever it was, she could handle it. I was going to stand guard in case anything else happened. I went and locked the door, just in case.

CHAPTER 62

ADAM

A knock at the door halted me. Who was still awake at this hour? The familiar blonde of Luna's hair shown in my shop light as she walked in, plopping a slack body on my table.

"Well, well, what did the cat drag in?" I asked, setting down what I had been working on. I needed to get something together to make all of these people forget what had happened. I didn't have the ingredients I wanted, but I could make do. It would just take a little longer. I didn't like tricking people, but it was safer for them to forget. It was the humane thing to do. Not that Cassandra had been thinking about what was humane at any point, apparently.

"Don't know," Luna said, shaking her head. "Melody found him at the doorstep just now."

I frowned. There sure were a lot of things landing on our doorstep in the last couple of hours. I wasn't sure how much more I could handle.

I listened for the boy's breath. His face looked like he had seen better days, both with meals, and, well…nearly anything else.

I turned on my overhead light, trying to get a better look. Pale skin shown back at me.

"Hmmm," I voiced. "Was he unconscious this whole time?"

I grabbed my wand to check for a tracker.

"Yeah," she affirmed. "He may just be another dumb kid who likes exploring abandoned places."

Pushing his sleeves and pants legs up, I searched for any signs of punctures or injures. My suspicions were confirmed when I found a tranq mark.

A rush of anxiety swam through my body. "If he's been tranqed, and he's here…then…"

CHAPTER 63

JAMES

My suit was torn.

I hadn't noticed on our way home, but as I stroked Titania's hair in a desperate attempt to get her to fall asleep, I saw the sleeve was sliced.

The fancy clothes shop was not going to be happy about this. What was I going to say? "Sorry I ruined your suit. I was off fighting bad guys—or girls, as the case may be." That might have been a bit melodramatic. Now that Cassandra wasn't going to be around anymore, one way or another, I wasn't sure how we were going to get funds. But that was a problem for in the morning. Not a problem for tonight.

Getting Titania to go to sleep was a monumental task after the night we had. I was honestly surprised when she had finally relaxed and dozed off. I took the opportunity to sneak into the kitchen to try to find some food. My stomach was about to start rumbling at any moment and I really didn't need her waking up.

The cabinet door creaked as I opened it in search of cereal. By the time I had poured myself a bowl, I was wondering if I should just go to bed myself. My eyelids were heavier than I could ever remember them being in my entire life.

I sat at the table, convincing myself that it was best to eat. I'd been through radiation poisoning, death-defying situations, a fight…I needed to make time to eat a second dinner. The carbs in that pasta from earlier had not lasted past the fight.

Then Titania screamed.

I jumped up, nearly knocking the bowl off the table as I ran to her bedside.

"What?" I called out as I rounded the corner, "What's wrong?"

She lay in the bed, her hands balled into fists right next to her face. I gently pushed her hands aside. Her eyes were closed, arms tense.

"Titania?" I asked. She didn't respond. She must've still been asleep.

I moved to rub her back, trying to calm her down. Today was a lot. Yesterday was a lot, too. And the day before that. Everything, really, had been a lot lately. We all needed a break.

Her whole body was rigid. I'd never seen anything like it before. I frowned, debating on waking her up. She'd been a wreck before we came home, talking a million miles an hour, worried that we weren't safe here or anywhere.

"It's okay," I whispered. "You're okay."

Her body contorted further and further into a ball. I decided to wake her up. This couldn't be good for her, whatever this was.

She shot up before I could start rousing her, screaming at the top of her lungs with her eyes wide open.

I jumped back.

She screamed until her voice cut off.

"Titania?" I asked, approaching her again, desperately hoping that she was actually awake this time.

She made eye contact with me, but didn't look like she recognized me. My stomach dove into the floorboards.

"Titania?" I tried again, my voice strained from trying to keep it steady.

Her shoulders relaxed.

She rubbed her eyes, trying to make things out in the dimly lit room. I rushed to flip on the light. I could see perfectly well in the moonlight, thanks to my three different sets of DNA, but I didn't know if hers provided her with any help with night vision.

"What was that?" I asked as she came to, her eyes briefly unfocused as she got her bearings.

"Nightmare," she mumbled.

Oh, yeah. She'd told me about her nightmares getting worse recently. I needed to ask Adam if there wasn't something she could take before bed to fix this. She was looking more and more tired every day.

"It's okay," I assured her, "I'm here."

"Yeah," she said, biting her lip. "Thank you."

"Anything for you…" I smiled, pressing my lips to her forehead. "Princess."

She groaned, playfully shoving me. My lip tilted upward.

There she was.

That was my girl.

COMING IN 2026...

METAMORPHOSIS

A crystal cave, untouched by time for years. Ice grew up to the ceiling, its glistening edges sharp and formidable. Metamorphosis had lost count early on of how many years she'd been trapped in their icy grip. It was cold, dark, and isolated. She wondered if she would ever see the sunlight again. But she knew she must. Everything came to an end eventually.

She had created her own hell. She wanted them to think she was dead. She didn't want to be hunted anymore. Those scientists were surely going to kill her...or put her in a prison of their own design. Guilt plagued her that she had asked for this. If only she had known what she was asking for.

She had only wanted her babies to survive. And in the end, she still didn't know if they had. They could be long dead, or they could be out, walking in the sunshine while she was stuck in a desolate cave.

Her enemies had tricked her, and she had fallen for it.

While she usually had no trouble changing every fiber of her being, choosing from the infinite options of what she could be, the ice kept her from being able to shift. And now she had to wait until it thawed. She wondered if she would look like she had aged. She wondered if she *had* aged. Not that it mattered. She could change her appearance however she wanted to. She'd gotten good at testing the limits of her abilities, being all alone in the wilderness. There wasn't much else to do, and she was curious. It wasn't like she could change the past. She had to embrace what was. What could be.

The claustrophobia of being trapped in this state for so long was wearing her thin. She could feel her sanity being pulled in a million different directions.

The only thing that she had to hang onto was the certainty that once she got out, she knew exactly where she was going.

She was going to find an old friend.

Silen.

And when she did, he wouldn't know what hit him.

Acknowledgments

It may take a village to raise a child, but it also takes one to bring a book into the world. I am blessed to have an amazing one!

Alway first and foremost being my husband, Thomas. He has always encouraged and enabled my creative pursuits, and this book was no different. Despite the challenges we've faced in the intervening years since Head Under Water, his support has given me the strength to move forward and come back for the characters I love.

I was so fortunate to be able to hire an editor for Haven. Not only is Holly of Bird and Bear Editing an amazing editor, she's also an amazing friend. Without her services and support, I don't know what I would have done.

And of course, I cannot forget Deranged Doctor Designs! Their covers are absolutely stunning, they are so wonderful to work with, and I will never stop recommending them.

Samuel C, my dragon-gifter who believed in the series so much that he funded the first three covers of Geneshifters. I cannot say thank you enough.

I also want to acknowledge my readers, who have stuck with me through thick and thin, sickness, natural disaster, and more. Thank you for being patient, understanding, and kind.

Finally, a big thank you to everyone who is helping with the launch of this book, leaving reviews, and telling their friends!

Thank you so much for reading!

If you'd like to go the extra mile, please consider leaving a review on your favorite review platform. :) It helps authors like me reach new readers!

ABOUT THE AUTHOR

Rebecca Lemke is a dystopian writer and author of the Geneshifters series. She spends her days dreaming of mythological shifters and scientific mad men. Rebecca loves exploring crises of identity, love, and morality in her books. When she's not writing, she can be found cosplaying her main character, sketching, hanging out with her loved ones, or cooking her favorite food, potatoes.

You can sign up for her email list here: https:// authorrebeccalemke.substack.com
Find her on social media at @authorrebeccalemke